Peter Never Came

Peter Never Came

Stories
by
Ashley Cowger

Autumn House Press Staff
Editor-in-Chief and Founder: Michael Simms
Executive Director: Richard St. John
Co-Founder: Eva-Maria Simms
Community Outreach Director: Michael Wurster
Fiction Editors: Sharon Dilworth, John Fried
Associate Editors: Ziggy Edwards, Erik Rosen, Rebecca King
Assistant Editor: Adrienne Block
Media Consultant: Jan Beatty
Publishing Consultant: Peter Oresick
Technology Consultant: Evan Oare
Tech Crew Chief: Michael Milberger
Intern: D. Gilson

PENNSYLVANIA ISBN: 978-1-932870-46-6
COUNCIL
ON THE Library of Congress Control Number: 2010915101

Autumn House Press receives state arts funding support through a grant from the Pennsylvania Council on the Arts, a state agency funded by the Commonwealth of Pennsylvania and the National Endowment for the Arts, a federal agency.

To Damien, more than anyone,

but also,

to the memory of Zooey, who was with me as I wrote all of these
stories,

and to Franny, who will be with me as I write many more.

Acknowledgements

Thanks to Sharon Dilworth, for believing in my manuscript and for helping me turn it into a book. Thanks, also, to Michael Simms and everyone else at Autumn House Press.

I owe a huge debt of gratitude to everyone affiliated with the University of Alaska Fairbanks MFA program during the time that I was there, especially Gerri Brightwell, David Crouse, Len Kamerling, Justus Humphrey, Shane Dayton, Melina Draper, Stu St. Croix, Lance Twitchell, Jenni Moody, and everyone else involved in David's novella workshop, which I still believe was the greatest workshop in the history of workshops.

Thanks, also, to Jayme Russell, Ike Oden, Mindy Armstrong, David Armstrong, and Jolynn Baldwin, for feedback and encouragement, and to my family, who have always somehow seemed to believe in me. And, of course, thanks to my husband, Damien, who gave me feedback on each story along the way, who went through the entire manuscript with me line-by-line, and whose love and support I simply could not do without.

Some of the stories in this collection were previously published (often in slightly different form) in the following journals: "8 Stories I'll Never Tell" originally appeared in *Pedestal*, "Shades of Blue" in *Bound Off*, "The Things We Take and the Things We Leave Behind" in *Fast Forward*, "What If You Married That Guy" in *Metal Scratches*, "Peter Never Came" in *Compass Rose*, and "The Number One" in *New Ohio Review*.

Table of Contents

Peter Never Came

PROLOGUE

8 STORIES I'LL NEVER TELL

There's a man—he's in his forties now—who each spring dons a new cap and gown, a shiny pair of black leather shoes, and walks in the local university's commencement ceremony. He never went to college himself, but he found out in a roundabout sort of way that the university doesn't double check those things: who is graduating and who isn't. All you have to do is put your name in and they'll announce you. Every year he chooses a different major, a different life he'll never live, and walks with the young and the ambitious. People applaud him, though nobody knows him there, and he looks out at the audience, tears gleaming in his eyes, and waves the rolled up piece of paper, which he knows by now without even looking reads in bold type, "This is not a diploma." He waves it at nobody, and nobody waves back. But I'll never tell his story. Someone will say he's too passive, not interesting enough, not taking an active role in his own empty life. And nobody wants to read about somebody like that.

There's an aging couple who never went to college, either. She became pregnant at sixteen and he did right by her and proposed, took an entry level job at a factory, gave up a football scholarship at the State University because, he knew, there was no future in that, anyway. Their kids—they ended up having three—are grown now, off making mistakes of their own. The financial burden is down to just the two of them, but two is enough these days. Two is more than enough. And while they know they'll never save enough to buy a home, they still scrape together their pennies, what little is left after rent and food and gas and insurance, to pay the rent on a storage unit that holds all the furniture and dishes and trinkets and things that they've accumulated over the years. Things they've been given as gifts or bought out of dreams of a future they would never have. Things they can't fit into their tiny, one bedroom apartment. But I'll never tell their story because someone will say that these two people will never grow. A couple too old, now, too set in their ways, to ever see that maybe it wasn't the things, all along, that made their lives worth living.

Or what about the woman who takes pictures of people who look happy? She brings her spy cam, a gift that she bought for her nephew but never gave, everywhere she goes and she snaps photos when she sees someone who is smiling or laughing or sitting on a bench contentedly feeding ducks. And she studies the pictures, studies the creases around the noses and mouths, the sparkle and glimmer in the eyes. She studies them and tries to see what it is that makes it happen. Standing in front of the mirror, she imitates the facial expressions, the bend and shape of the lips and the angle of the head to the body. But she never quite seems to get it right, so she keeps taking more and more photos, every day, and searches for the link between them all. I'll never tell her story because someone will say it is too hard to care about someone so far off track, someone who thinks the secret to happiness lies in the wrinkles around a stranger's smile.

And I'll never tell the story of the woman so selfless she gives all but the bare essentials of her paycheck to the homeless, because she has no flaws, that I can see, and someone will say people that true of heart couldn't exist in a world such as this. And I won't tell about the man who drinks one warm cup of tea on the first of every month, and he waits for the first of every month like a child waits for Christmas, because someone will point out that personal deprivation does not make a difference in the bigger picture. I won't tell of the woman who wears her hair a different way every day just so that she can believe things can change, or the man who hasn't seen his own parents in seven years because he thinks he will be a disappointment to them now. Or the millions and millions of people, groping blindly in the darkness, trying to find their way.

PART ONE: PAN

SHADES OF BLUE

Everybody wore blue to Tommy Dilman's funeral. They wore blue because it had been Tommy's favorite color and because Megan Dilman, Tommy's mom, insisted that it was less sad that way. Less like mourning Tommy's death and more like celebrating his life. So everybody wore blue because Megan said they had to, and nobody wanted to upset Megan any further. But most of the mourners who crowded into the small sanctuary wore navy blues and dark dark blues, blues so deep they may as well have been black. Megan, though, wore powder blue, baby blue, the blue of a temperate sky. And she wore a summer dress that was at least two sizes too small, as was evidenced by the froth colored flesh oozing around each spaghetti strap and spilling over the edges at the top. Everybody said she looked radiant, lovely. They said she looked just like she had ten years before.

The dress was, in fact, from that era of Megan's life, the time before the baby fat and the exhaustion. She had been hanging on to it all these years in the hopes that she might one day be able to wear it again. It was, after all, her favorite summer dress, and having it hanging in her closet served as a constant reminder of how she had once looked, how she could look again if she just got around to losing the weight. And she had lost some of it, almost fifteen pounds, but it had come off slowly,

11

two or three pounds a year. And she still couldn't fit into that pale blue spaghetti strap dress, not well, not so that she actually looked right in it.

The fact that she had chosen to wear it even though she couldn't really pull it off, well, nobody could quite decide what it meant. Was it because it was the only thing she owned that was just the right shade of blue? Was it some sort of statement about starting over, about setting the clock back? They argued about it afterwards, when they went home to their own still alive children, when they were no longer face to face with the strangely serene smile that Megan turned on every single person as they stepped through the sanctuary's double doors.

"So glad you could come," she said to each of them and smiled. "Tommy would be happy to know that so many people cared."

Of course it wasn't for Tommy that most of them were there. It was for Megan, and even then it was partly just for the sake of it. Because it was a small town and Tommy was a six-year-old boy. Because nothing brings people together like a tragedy.

And anyway, a typical six-year-old boy hasn't done much to affect the lives of an entire town's worth of people, even a town as small as this. A six-year-old boy plays cops and robbers in his backyard; he throws rocks at the windows of passing cars and then cries when he hears the crash; he flies kites that get tangled in the limbs of tall trees.

And Tommy was the most typical of six-year-old boys. The sort that nobody's aware of until he climbs to the top of the Southwark Creek Bridge and dives head first into the shallow water. Tommy was the sort of boy who seemed more there in his absence than he ever had when he had actually been around. But since he wasn't around anymore, he was no longer a typical six-year-old boy. He was a dead six-year-old boy, and that turned him into something magical and heartbreaking. The stuff of small town legends.

And so most everybody in the town showed up to the tiny church and filed one by one into the stuffy sanctuary, pausing to shake hands with Megan, who nobody had expected to be greeting them at the entrance. "I'm so sorry for your loss, Megan," they said, or, "Tommy was a remarkable little boy."

And Megan smiled with off-putting tranquility as she squeezed their hands and patted their shoulders and said, "He would be so happy to know you came," over and over and over again.

At least the rest of the family—Tommy's dad, Hank, and Tommy's grandparents: the widow Martin, and Grandma and Grandpa Dilman—all looked solemn. Grammie Martin was even crying, which was comforting, somehow. That's the way you're supposed to be, the people of the town each thought to themselves. Not dressed in light light blue and smiling. You were supposed to be beside yourself with grief because it was tragic, the death of this boy who could have grown up to be anything. An astronaut. The president. A brilliant scientific mind.

It was tragic, of course, because nobody knew what Tommy Dilman would have grown up to become. They didn't know that in a few years he would have gotten a girl pregnant—a fourteen-year-old girl, and he only age thirteen—and immediately after denying his role in the whole thing, he would have gone to live with his Grammie for a while. Nobody would ever know that during his stay with Grammie Martin, Tommy would have thrown raucous parties, all but obliterating his grandmother's house, and that he would eventually have snuck off one night, at age sixteen, taking his grandmother's debit and credit cards with him.

And nobody knew, either, that Tommy Dilman would have burned down his Grandma and Grandpa Dilman's farm in a drunken rage one evening, had he lived. At age twenty-seven, during a visit, Tommy would have gotten into an argument with his Grandpa, and, in a childish attempt at having the last word, Tommy would have set fire to the fields and then to the farmhouse itself, before taking off in his grandparents' truck. The truck would have been recovered—the next day, totaled in a ditch on the side of the highway—but the farm would have been lost forever.

But now these things would never be, just like Tommy Dilman would never zero out the college fund that his parents started for him at his birth, spending all the money on CDs and marijuana. Now his parents wouldn't have to one day hear the news that their son has been arrested for not making his child support payments—for another child, a second child who the Dilmans wouldn't even have known about—or that their son is under suspicion for an email scam, in which he contacted several thousand strangers and asked them to donate money so he could treat his fictional cancer.

Not knowing the things that never would now come to be, everybody took their seats at Tommy Dilman's funeral thinking of the things that had been, the things that would be no longer. Images of a little boy playing ball at the park. A five-year-old with pockets full of halves of inchworms because he had learned that you could chop them just so in the middle and they would become two living worms instead of one. The time Tommy shoplifted a handful of gummy bears from the Grab 'N' Bag, and then, fraught with the guilt of it, vomited them up in a colorful mess in the parking lot. A giddy six-year-old boy jumping from the swing set at the crest of his upswing so that he could fly as high as he could go, could reach his peak, before being pulled once again back down to the ground.

BOY SCOUT FINN

You don't know me unless you read about Michael and my dad and all that in the paper. But that's why I wanted to write this down, 'cause all that stuff they said in the paper and on the news, it wasn't really true, most of it, and nobody ever even asked my side of what happened. My name's Finneas. My dad named me that, after my great grampa who I never met 'cause he wasn't alive anymore when I was born. But nobody ever calls me Finneas, 'cept my Nonna and Grandaddy, but they don't really count 'cause they live out in California and we don't ever go there 'cept on vacation.

Everybody just calls me Finn, and some people, the activists or whatever they are, those guys call me Boy Scout Finn 'cause they say it's like that book, Huckleberry Finn, which my dad says was written by Mark Twain, but I know it was written by Huckleberry himself. He says it right in the book. I know 'cause I read it even though the librarian at my school, she told me it was probably out of my age group. And Miss Marshall, she's the librarian I told you about, she told me it was written by a man named Samuel Clemens but like I said, both her and my dad must never have read it 'cause Huckleberry says that he wrote it all himself and that it's a lot of work, writing a book, and I think he's probably right so I'm gonna keep this short.

But anyway, that stuff doesn't really matter. What matters is that it isn't true, that stuff they said in the paper about Michael.

15

They mostly just wanted to know what my dad thought about it all, 'cause he was the one pressing charges. That one reporter from the TV asked me what all I thought about it but I was kinda nervous 'cause there were three cameras on me and the lights were really bright and my dad was all looking at me like "don't mess this up for us, Finn," and so I just said how I thought Michael was a really good Scout Master, which he was, and how I didn't really understand all this stuff about homosexuals and all.

All I really know about it is that Michael's a homosexual and my dad says that's a bad thing. But I don't know what it means, otherwise than that, 'cause nobody will tell me when I ask. My dad told me it was like a kid in the candy store, having a homosexual working with the Scouts, but I didn't really get that 'cause there's this candy store at the mall and the only ones who ever go there are kids. But it was like my dad was saying homosexuals don't belong in the Boy Scouts, so I didn't much understand that part, but anyway, my dad says that homosexuals are bad and that they're not supposed to be around kids.

But it's weird 'cause when Michael took over as our Scout Master everyone was all saying how much better he was than our old Scout Master, whose name is Mr. Frank. I didn't like Mr. Frank much, partly 'cause he made us call him Mr. Frank and Michael always let us call him Michael. But Mr. Frank was loud, too, always yelling and stuff. He used to be an army man, and he said how the Boy Scouts was supposed to be good preparation for joining the army. But I don't think I want to, if you have to yell all the time and tell people that they have to call you Mr. Frank or sir. Sometimes he had us call him sir.

Michael was way more fun than Mr. Frank from the start, and everybody thought so, even my dad. The very first day Michael came on as Scout Master, he had us all play this game about how to respect other people. We stood around in a circle and we were supposed to look at each other and say things about what kind of person the boy on either side of us looked like he'd be and it was all kinds of fun 'cause I knew the people on either side of me real well and I knew they weren't much like what they looked like they'd be. Like, when it came my turn I said that Mark, who was on my left side, looked like his mom cut his hair for him, even though I knew that he got that haircut on purpose from an actual barber. And I said that probably meant he was super poor and needed us to donate money to him. Everyone laughed 'cause Mark's the richest kid in the Troop, pretty much.

And then after we all went around and said what we thought each other looked like, Michael asked us what all we thought the game had taught us. Well this guy Toby Mendellson said how it taught us that you can't judge a book by its cover and Michael said yes, that's right, but then I said that it also taught us that just 'cause you think there's something weird about somebody or 'cause they're different from you, that doesn't mean there's anything wrong with them or that they even are actually any different, and Michael said how I was right, too, but I'm pretty sure my answer was righter than Toby's 'cause I'm smart and Toby doesn't know much outside of fishing, which he does every weekend with his grampa.

And anyway, that first day Michael taught us about wilderness survival. He said how it was a carnival rule of scouting, knowing how to make it out in the woods, and he told us we should decide what three things we would bring with us if we were going out into the wilderness and why. When it came my turn, I told Michael I would bring a tent, so I could have a place to sleep, and I would bring my pocket knife, for protection and also to cut up the food I find and what all, and then I said since that was all I would really need to survive, I would also bring a magnifying glass.

17

"How come the magnifying glass?" Michael wanted to know.

"'Cause," I said, "it would probably get boring out there all by myself."

"Yes," Michael said. "But how come not an Ipod or something like that?"

Everyone kinda snickered and I felt my cheeks get hot but I kept going, anyway. "I like music," I said. "And I like reading, too, and video games. But if I could only bring one other thing with me, I think I'd want the magnifying glass 'cause I would probably want to take things apart and look at them up closer. There's a lot of things you could look at through a magnifying glass in the woods."

Michael smiled and said how that was an excellent answer, and then we moved on, but afterwards, when I was waiting for my dad to pick me up, Michael put his hand on my shoulder and told me that the magnifying glass was a really special kind of answer and how he could tell I was a really special kind of boy.

"I like looking at things up close too," he told me. "And it takes a special person to be able to say something different from everyone else."

My dad pulled up and honked the horn and I told Michael how I hadda go 'cause my dad's real tired on Wednesdays and he wants to go straight home and put me to bed so he can have some quiet. Michael walked to the car with me and bent down to lean in the window and talk to my dad.

"There a problem?" my dad asked.

"Not at all. Just thought I'd introduce myself. Michael. I'm the new Scout Master." Michael reached his hand into the window and shook hands with my dad. "Finn is a remarkable boy."

My dad laughed. "Yeah. Right."

Michael's eyebrows went up but he didn't say anything else, just turned to me and waved.

"That your new Scout Master?" my dad asked on the way home, even though Michael had already told him who he was.

"Yep."

"Seems like a good man," my dad said. "He's got a firm handshake. Never trust a man without a firm handshake, Finn."

But now my dad acts like he never said anything like that, and he says how there were warning signs from day one, but I remember that first day and how happy my dad was about Michael and his handshake and the fact that I liked him so much better than Mr. Frank.

Anyway, things were going really well with Michael at the Scouts and pretty much everybody liked him, seemed to me. But this one day when we came in to start the meeting, a bunch of the parents came in with us, even my dad, which I thought was weird 'cause he never usually comes to Scout meetings with me, just drops me off and then picks me up after.

There was this man, who I think is in charge in some way but I'm not really sure how, he led Michael up to the front and then kept standing there right behind him. He was wearing a suit, the man, and a tie and everything, and the look on his face was super serious and kinda mean and I thought how if we had a Scout Master like him I would just quit.

"Well, Scouts," Michael said, and then looked back at the man.

The man nodded.

Michael looked back at us. "I've had such a great time these past few months with you boys and I'm going to miss you all so much."

And you could hear all these gasps and mumbles coming from the Troop 'cause that was the first we realized what was going on, that Michael was leaving.

19

"But I'm going to be leaving you tonight and you'll have a new Scout Master starting next week."

"Why, Michael?" one of the boys, I think it was Joey, asked.

"Well," Michael said, but the man behind him stepped forward and talked over him. Michael kept talking at first and I tried to listen to him but the other man was talking so much louder I couldn't hear, so Michael just stopped and let the man go.

"Mr. Phillips here would have loved to keep working with you boys, but he recognizes that he's not an appropriate authority figure for you." The man looked over at Michael, but Michael didn't nod or agree or disagree or anything.

"But we like Michael," Mickey called, and the rest of us nodded in agreement.

"Boys, I . . ." But the man started talking over Michael again and Michael gave up right away this time.

"Michael really enjoyed his time here but he needs to move on now and you boys can rest assured that we'll find a suitable replacement."

And they wouldn't tell us anything more. It wasn't until I got home that I found out about Michael being a homosexual and all. My dad was super mad about it, and that's how come I left. I wasn't kidnapped, like my dad says, I left on my own 'cause my dad was so mad and I didn't want to be around him anymore. He was saying mean things about my friend. Michael was my friend and I know he's a homosexual, and I guess homosexuals aren't supposed to be around kids, but Michael was nicer to me than Mr. Frank was, and he's nicer than my dad too. And I know it's wrong, what I did next, but that's okay, 'cause I think I'd rather be wrong than yell all the time, like Mr. Frank does, or get mad over little things that don't much seem to matter, like my dad does.

My dad was just raving at me that night, super angry and asking me, "Did Michael ever touch you? Did he ask you to touch him?"

What a stupid question. You can't be a Scout Master without at least brushing shoulders with the Scouts and you wouldn't be a good Scout Master if you didn't pat the Scouts on the back now and then, which is something Mr. Frank woulda never done and that's why he wasn't a very good Scout Master in my opinion. But I could tell it was supposed to be real bad if Michael touched me, so I said, "No, dad, he never touched any of us." And I know it's wrong to lie but my dad's eyes were bulging out of their sockets and he was pacing back and forth super fastly and I was just trying to calm him down.

"Because so help me, if he touched you . . ." And he leaned down and put his hands on my shoulders, squeezed really hard and shook me.

"He didn't touch me," I said again, and he let go of me and I had to rub where he had squeezed me 'cause it was super sore and that's when I decided I had to get out of there. My dad was acting crazy and I didn't know what he might do but I wasn't gonna stick around to find out.

I figured I would go out into the woods 'cause I had already gotten three merit badges that would help me out there. I know how to light a fire without a lighter and I know how to tell which berries are probably poisoned and everything. I figured I could live out there forever, or at least 'til I turned eighteen and I could come back without having to stay with my dad anymore.

Thanks to Michael, I knew exactly what all to pack to survive in the wilderness and I had a tent that my dad gave me last Christmas for when I wanted to go camping in the back yard. I waited 'til my dad was asleep and then I snuck out the back door with my tent, my sleeping bag, my pocket knife, and my magnifying glass. I know Michael said you're only supposed

21

to take three things but I could fit the sleeping bag inside the tent so it was kind of like they were one thing, really.

There's a park just a few blocks away from my house and I knew I could probably stay there for a while without anyone noticing me 'cause it was a big park and there were lots of trees and nobody much goes to the park in my town. The street lights were just coming on as I walked down the sidewalk and the sky was all purple and pink, so I knew that if anyone drove by and saw me they'd probably want to know what I was doing out so late on my own. But nobody did 'cause it's a quiet place, our town, and people don't usually stay out much later than the sun, not in our neighborhood, anyway.

When I got there I pitched up my tent the way Michael taught us but I started to feel kinda scared 'cause it was getting dark fast and my dad usually leaves the hall light on for me. He always leaves my door open a crack too. Where I was, at the back of the park by the trees, the streetlights weren't really shining over there. Plus there were noises, twigs snapping and leaves rustling, and I thought what if there were wolves or something in the park? But I remembered that I knew where Michael lived 'cause we had a potluck in his back yard one time and it wasn't very far from the park, either.

So I took down my tent and I did it slow and proper, even though the noises were getting louder and I really wanted to get out of there, 'cause Michael told us that if you're in too much of a hurry when you take your tent down you'll probably rip it. Then I bundled everything up again and walked over to Michael's house.

When I got there, he had his front porch light on and his car wasn't in the driveway so I figured he must not be home, but that was okay 'cause he had taught us all the tricks on where you should hide your spare key so no one will find it. I checked a few places and then found it, buried under a little bit of soil in his flower garden.

So I let myself in and went into the living room. I figured Michael wouldn't mind if I spent the night down there 'cause his bedroom was upstairs anyway and I'd explain everything to him as soon as he got home from wherever he was at. I laid my sleeping bag out on the couch and climbed into it and I fell asleep pretty fastly 'cause I guess I was real tired.

When I woke up I didn't really know what was going on. I didn't remember where I was and it was real loud 'cause somebody was banging on the front door. I heard someone walking down the stairs, and I was scared. So I kinda bunched myself real low into my sleeping bag and pulled it over my head. Even though I'm not dumb and I know just 'cause you can't see them doesn't mean they can't see you, I still felt safer not looking at whatever was coming to get me.

The light flicked on and inside my sleeping bag everything became all red, 'cause my sleeping bag is red, you see. And then I heard the front door open and Michael's voice sounding all tired. "Can I help you?" That was when I remembered where I was and why.

"You tell me," a deep voice said.

"Give me back my son, you bastard!" That one was my dad, I could tell right away, and I realized that I was gonna get in major trouble.

"Excuse me?" Michael asked.

"Give him back, you faggot."

There was a scuttling sound and then the man with the deep voice said, "Whoa, whoa. Back up."

"Can somebody please tell me what the hell this is about?" That was Michael.

"This gentleman here claims his son disappeared and that there's reason to suspect he might be here."

"I know he's here!"

23

As you can imagine, I felt kinda embarrassed 'cause I hadn't thought my dad would find me so easily, plus, I didn't want Michael to get in trouble. I slinked further down into my sleeping bag and hoped that nobody would notice I was there.

"Finn is gone?" Michael asked.

There was another scuttling sound and you could hear everybody yelling, my dad at Michael, Michael for my dad to get off of him, and then the other man for everybody to just calm down, please just calm down and let's figure this thing out.

When the ruckus stopped, Michael said, "You can search my place if you want. He isn't here."

"That would be great," the man with the deep voice said.

I heard footsteps moving around and then somebody pulled open the top of my sleeping bag and unzipped it enough so they could see my face. I squinted into the bright light and saw my dad, looking all angry, and then I saw the police officer, and I knew right away that's what he was 'cause he was wearing a uniform and a badge. And then I saw Michael. His forehead was all wrinkly, and his eyes were cloudy and confused.

"I knew it," my dad said and he yanked me out of the sleeping bag by the arm. It hurt so bad I thought my arm was going to pull clear off but it didn't, and before I had a chance to explain what had happened my dad was yelling at Michael again. "You sick pervert! Fucking faggot!" (I know I'm not supposed to use the F word, and usually I don't, but I'm just telling you what it was my dad said.)

"Can you explain what the boy is doing asleep in your living room?" the officer asked.

"I . . . I don't know," Michael said. He looked from the officer to my dad to me.

"Son?" The officer turned to me and kneeled down, putting his hands on his knees and tilting his head. His voice went all

24

high pitched and whiny and he said, "Can you tell us what you're doing here?"

And I was about to say but then my dad started yelling again. He ran and grabbed Michael and punched him in the face and the officer hadda run over and pull my dad off of Michael and then the officer said for my dad to take me home and that he would call us in the morning.

My dad didn't give me a chance to grab my stuff, and I could tell he was super mad on the drive home so I didn't ask him about going back for it. And then the next day he took me down to the police station and he told me to tell them all about how Michael had kidnapped me and all the ways Michael had touched me, even though Michael hadn't touched me or kidnapped me or anything.

"Well," I said, but before I could say anything else my dad started to talk over me.

"This man came to our house at night and kidnapped my son, right under my nose, and brought him back to his house," my dad said.

"Did he touch you, son?" the officer asked me.

"Well," I said, but my dad interrupted me again.

"The man's got them so accustomed to his abuse they don't even recognize it as abuse anymore," he said.

The officer wrote down everything my dad said and then my dad's lawyer read it at the trial like I had said that stuff, which I hadn't. And Michael wouldn't hardly look at me and I thought maybe they would let me talk, ask for my side of what happened, but nobody ever did and before I knew it the trial was over and Michael was going away to jail.

Afterwards, my dad took me out for ice cream and told me about how he was sorry if that bad man had messed my mind up and how he would never let anything like that happen to me again. It was weird, 'cause it was the first time my dad had taken me out for ice cream in a long time and I wasn't sure if I should be happy about that or sad about how Michael was going to be locked away for a very long time, probably, and all 'cause of what I did.

And then after that, the people from the paper came around and then that guy from the TV came and wanted to talk to us about what had happened, and they wanted to know what all Michael had done to me and whether or not I agreed with my dad. And then people started saying how my dad was the one warping my mind and how he was leading me and stuff like that, and even though I don't really understand what all they meant, I think they were kinda right 'cause my dad hardly ever lets me give my side of the story and that's why I had to write it all down, 'cause otherwise I can't seem to get it out right.

All I know is what all I can tell you, and that's that I left 'cause my dad was mad and I went to Michael's 'cause I like Michael and I thought he would help me. And ever since Michael left the Scouts, a bunch of us boys haven't even wanted to go anymore. The new Scout Master might not be as bad as Mr. Frank, but he's not as nice or fun or funny as Michael, even though he's not a homosexual. His name is Evan and he talks like he always has a cold and he wears glasses and he can't even start a fire without a match. I know 'cause he tried to demonstrate it and he couldn't do it. And that wouldn't even be so bad, 'cept that he talks to us like we're little kids and he always acts like everything any of us says is dumb.

And things aren't as fun at the Scouts without Michael anyway, 'cause the other kids are all acting like they never liked Michael either, which I know is a lie 'cause we were all upset when we found out he was leaving. This one time we were playing bank robbery, and Toby was the robber and I was the cop and Mark was the teller and everybody else was the customers. And

Toby came up with his gun already pulled, and he told Mark how he better give him the money or he was gonna shoot up the place.

I came storming in to arrest Toby and save the day, and Toby said, all mad, "You can't come yet, Finn, nobody called you. You don't even know about the robbery!"

And I said, "Yeah-huh, 'cause I was coming into the bank anyway to make a deposit."

"Nuh-uh! That's not allowed," Toby said.

And Mark said, "Yeah-huh it is. He's one of my regular customers. He comes in here every morning at this time."

And everybody all agreed how that seemed fair but Toby didn't like it much, and then he threw his gun on the ground and it became a stick again and he stomped on it, so it's a good thing it wasn't a real gun 'cause it woulda probably gone off and killed us all. And then he said, "You guys are all a buncha homos!"

I was so mad 'cause even though I don't really know what makes you a homosexual, I don't think it has anything to do with the way you handle a bank robbery or whether or not you go to the bank at the same time every morning, and Toby was saying it like it was the meanest insult you could give and I don't know but being like Michael wouldn't be so bad in my eyes. Before I really knew what I was doing, I jumped on Toby and punched him three or four times square in the jaw, and then Evan came and pulled me off and said how he was going to call my dad and I would have to go home and he didn't know if I would be allowed to come back. But I don't really care 'cause the Scouts are no fun without Michael anyway.

My dad was real mad about it all and said how I shoulda thought about the cons 'n' questions, 'cause now he had to figure out what to do with me on Wednesday nights since that's the

27

night he goes to play poker with his friends. And he said that I'm real lucky that Toby's mom didn't press charges, 'cause she coulda and I woulda gone to juvie.

But I don't care about any of that. See, I know it was wrong to hit Toby and I know it's wrong, too, to write this. My dad will be real mad if they decide to put it in the paper. But if I can help get Michael out of jail I'll do it 'cause I think it's wrong, too, putting somebody in jail for something he didn't do, even if he is a homosexual. And anyway, I think I like Michael better than my dad, and better than Evan and Mr. Frank.

Well I guess that's about all I have to say. You can make of it what you will. I just wanted to tell my side of what happened and I know I'm gonna get in a lot of trouble when my dad sees this, and I know I probably deserve it, but I don't feel bad about one word of any of it. Only thing I feel bad about is getting Michael put in jail and, right or wrong, that's the truth.

THE END. YOURS TRULY, FINN.

PAN AND PIRATES

Hugh Furlong tells people that the single, snapshot moment that's been burned into his brain to mark the end of his childhood was the moment he saw his brother Peter's fist make contact with Albert Frank's jaw. The moment he heard that soft thud and then the crack, as if something had been broken that could never be replaced. That moment, he says, meant more to him than when he punched Albert, too. Meant more than the phone call from Mrs. Frank, telling Peter and Hugh's mom that Albert was in the hospital and guess who had put him there? More than Hugh's three months in juvie—Peter's stint was longer, a full year, because he was older and so, they said, should have known better—or the first few days back at school after, when the other kids in second grade and even the teachers all looked at Hugh different, like they didn't know him anymore.

Hugh tells people that that was the moment, but it isn't really true. Partly because there can't just be one moment, can there? One single instant that is the definitive instant that draws the line between boy and man. But mostly because, even if there was a moment like that, for Hugh Furlong it would have happened before that fight. By that moment, by the time Peter's fist smashed into Albert's jaw, Hugh the boy was already gone.

During morning recess that day, Peter had told Hugh about the rumor that had been spreading around the school like

29

an infectious disease and which Albert Frank had personally started. Peter had clasped onto Hugh's elbow and looked him solemnly in the eyes when he told him, and that's how Hugh knew it was something bad. He didn't, otherwise, know what the word meant.

"What does it mean?" he asked Peter. "Something to do with eating insects, right?"

"Not exactly," Peter said, but he apparently didn't want to elaborate any further.

Hugh hadn't known at the time about Peter's dad—about what he had done to Peter when he thought nobody would catch them. If he had known, Hugh probably would have let it drop, but instead he asked Peter, "But it's a insult, right?"

"Yes," Peter said. His jaw tensed and his lips grew thin and taught. "It's meant as an insult. And what are we going to do about it?"

Hugh asked his brother, "What would Pan do?" which was sort of their mantra. Words to live by. Their mom had told them once that if they ever needed help figuring out the right thing to do, they should just ask themselves, "What would Jesus do?" When they discussed it later both boys agreed that whatever the answer to the question would be, it wasn't likely to be very interesting or worth doing. "Besides," Peter had added, "I don't think it's a good idea to follow the footsteps of someone whose choices in life got him put to death by the government. I'm not saying he didn't do the right things, but I'd rather do things that won't get me killed, if you want to know the truth." They decided that a much wiser and more pleasurable course of action would be to figure out what Peter Pan would do and then follow his actions exactly.

Peter Pan was Peter's favorite book back then, for obvious reasons, and as a result, it was Hugh's favorite book, too, though Hugh couldn't actually read it yet, and had to have Peter read it aloud to him. Peter said it had been his dad's favorite book also, and that his dad had named him after Pan, although their mom said it wasn't true. Said Peter was named after some soap opera star, but Peter didn't believe it. Deep down inside he knew the truth. He was the boy who would never grow old. All of Hugh and Peter's games revolved around the Pan characters in some way or another, and their favorite game, Pan and Pirates—their own makeshift version of Cowboys and Indians—had even begun to catch on with some of the other kids at school.

"Well," Peter said, "first of all Pan'd probably ambush Albert or something. And then he'd taunt him and make everyone laugh at him."

Hugh nodded. "Pan'd probably call on somebody else to help him out."

"I have an idea," Peter said, and took off towards the boys' room.

Hugh chased after him. When he got inside he had to pause, let his eyes adjust to the flickering fluorescent light. "What?" he asked Peter, and then again, "What?"

"Shh," Peter said, and then walked down the line of stalls, kicking in the doors to make sure nobody else was there. When the last stall proved vacant, he walked back to the front of the bathroom, to the row of sinks and the mirror above them. "I know who we can get to help us."

"Who?" Hugh asked.

Peter flicked off the lights.

Hugh's heart began to throb. "Peter, who? I can't see anything."

"Give it a second. Your eyes'll adjust," Peter said.

And he was right; after a few seconds, the grey forms inside the bathroom came into a shadowy focus. There were the stalls, and the mile long, filthy, cloth roll towel, hanging down

31

from its metal container in a loose loop. There were the sinks and counter, and, above them, the mirror. Everything was cast in shades of grey but it was all visible now and that, at least, was something.

Hugh folded his arms. "Okay, but it's still pretty dark."

"I know," Peter said. "But it has to be completely dark or else he won't come."

"Who won't come? Peter, what's going on?"

"Look into the mirror," Peter said in a solemn tone.

Hugh did, and a vague version of himself stared back. "Okay."

"What do you see?"

"I see myself."

"Really look," Peter said.

Hugh leaned in further toward the glass and squinted. "I see myself, Peter. Just myself."

Peter sighed. "I'm going to tell you a story. About the evil pirate in the land of the mirrors."

"The land of the mirrors." Hugh had meant it to sound skeptical, but it came out with a touch of awe.

"His name is Angus," Peter said. "Angus D. Firebelly. The D stands for Develish. What happened was Angus was doing his thing, you know: raping and pillaging, and cooking and eating small children."

"Yick."

"And Captain Jaz. Hook, none other, felt threatened, because Angus was a much better pirate than he and it is commonly believed that Angus could have killed Pan like that," Peter snapped, "if he ever set his mind to it."

"How come I've never heard of him before?" Hugh asked.

"Well he isn't in the book or anything. J. M. Barrie left that part out because it was too scary."

"How come you know about him then?"

"Because. I met Angus right here in this very bathroom. He told me his whole story. About how Jaz. and his pirates ambushed him. They killed off his entire crew and then did a magical incantation to trap him forever in the land of the mirrors. He's been trapped in there for ages. He can only come out whenever someone recites the right words, and even then he can only stay out for a short period of time. But what havoc he can wreak in that short period."

"You called him out before?" Hugh asked.

"No," Peter said. "I never had reason to. He tried to get me to, though. Told me he would do all kinds of favors for me if I just let him out for a little while. But I wasn't sure because he's got such a reputation and he *is* the evilest of all the pirates."

Hugh took a deep breath and looked more closely at the mirror. He could make out his and Peter's images well enough, but behind them was a spray of indistinguishable figures. Leaning against the back wall was what may be a mop, but may be something more—a tall and slender pirate—and in the darkened, shady mirror, the long, looping cloth roll towel looked almost human, too.

"Peter," Hugh said, and his voice came out shaky and small. "I don't want to play this game." He turned to walk over to the door, but Peter put a hand on his shoulder. Peter's fingers felt icy, like the darkness around them had penetrated deep inside him. When Hugh looked back at Peter, he could almost believe that it had. That there was something in the shadows that had possessed his brother. There was something in the shadows and it was coming, now, for Hugh.

"But Hugh," Peter said, "it isn't a game."

33

Hugh looked back at the towel and the mop in the mirror. "If he's a evil pirate, how can we know he won't kill us instead of Albert? Or kill all three of us?"

Peter shook his head. "That's just the thing, isn't it? We can't know. But you know, Pan says that to die would be a very great adventure."

Hugh stepped up to the counter and braced himself against the edge. "What do we do?"

"Look into your reflection, Hugh. Look hard."

Hugh stared into the mirror. The whites of his eyes caught what little light there was in the room, and they seemed to be glowing.

"Keep staring at your own reflection as I say the magical words."

"Then what will happen?"

"You'll notice him slowly materializing over your image. And don't be afraid, Hugh. He's scary looking, but I won't let him out of the mirror until he promises to help us with Albert."

Hugh's forehead was beginning to sweat and he reached up with his forearm to swipe it clean.

"Are you looking hard into your reflection?" Peter asked.

"Yes."

"Angus," Peter said. "Oh hear our solemn plea. Angus Develish Firebelly, come to us from beyond."

Hugh stared into the glowing whites of his reflection's eyes. The image seemed to shimmer and morph in front of him, the darkness edged in around the contours of his face but when he looked from the eyes to the edges around his reflection's face, he saw that nothing had changed. Hugh looked back at the eyes. He thought for a second that they flashed a different color, but in the darkness it was so hard to tell. His stomach was cold and the hair on his arms and legs stood on end. He wanted to ask Peter to stop, please stop. Angus was on his way; Hugh could feel it in the air, in his stomach, in his blood. Angus would soon overtake Hugh's reflection and Hugh didn't want to watch it happen, to watch his own face transform into something unfamiliar.

"Angus Develish Firebelly," Peter chanted. His voice was so low it almost sounded like a growl and it seemed to come not from his body, but from his soul. "Angus Develish Firebelly," he said, a little louder. "Angus!" he yelled. "Develish! Firebelly!"

Peter stopped talking and Hugh kept staring at his reflection. It looked ghastly in the dim light, with its glowing eyes and murky edges. It lived in the shadows—this being, this beast—and though it still looked like Hugh, not Angus D. Firebelly, it was an evil other version of Hugh. It was sinister, mysterious, magical.

As Hugh stared into his reflection a thick silence filled the air. There was no sound but for his and Peter's heavy breathing, and after a second even that faded into the background. The blood beat in Hugh's ears and all he could hear for a moment was that thump, thump, thump. Hugh's reflection's teeth glinted and for a moment Hugh felt certain that the transformation was complete. He drew his top lip down over his teeth and watched as his reflection did the same. Not complete yet. But that face glaring back at him: it was hard. The skin didn't look soft the way Hugh's skin was soft. Where Hugh's features were round and elastic, his reflection's features appeared fixed, unyielding.

Hugh fought the urge to close his eyes. He felt certain that if he closed his eyes now, he would be locked forever in this state somewhere between boy and pirate. He focused hard on the eyes inside the mirror. Looked as intently as he had ever looked at anything.

And then nothing.

And then nothing.

And then the door creaked open, the light flicked back on. And then, a cool flood of relief.

The boys looked up at Mr. Harnsworth, the janitor, looking down at them. "What you gents doing in yere, eh?"

"Nothing," Peter said quickly. "Just playing a game."

Harnsworth jangled his enormous ring of keys on his belt loop. "Bell rang a'ready."

"Sorry, sir. We didn't hear it in here."

Harnsworth motioned his head toward the door. "A'right. A'right. But get go'n, now."

Peter and Hugh hurried out of the bathroom, looking down.

Years later, after the rumor and the fight and the consequences of both had receded deeply into the past, Hugh and Peter reunited after years of unintended separation to visit Peter's dad's funeral. Not because they loved him—they didn't, they hadn't even known the man—but because Peter felt compelled somehow, compelled was the only way he could describe it, and he needed Hugh to come along.

Hugh was thirty-five and Peter almost forty, and both men had been in and out of jail most of their lives for things like petty theft and drugs, and in Peter's case, assault. They hadn't actually seen each other in almost seven years, but when Peter called Hugh and told him that his dad had died—liver failure, apparently he was a drunk, Peter said—Hugh understood at once that there are certain bonds that cannot be untied, and brotherhood is one of them.

There was hardly anybody at the funeral, which seemed to comfort Peter. "I don't know why," he said, "but I think it would bother me if he had turned out to be Mr. Popularity or something, or if there were a bunch of other sons and daughters here."

Hugh nodded. They sat in silence through the service as the pastor stumbled his way through generalized details about Peter's father's life. After the service, Peter and Hugh made their way up to the casket to take a look at the man who had done things to Peter that Peter couldn't even remember. Neither Hugh nor Peter actually knew what Peter's father had looked like in life, so they couldn't say whether he looked just as he always had, like he was just sleeping, but they could say he didn't look scary or imposing or mean or perverted, all descriptions their mother would have attached to him. He just looked small inside the giant pine box. Small and kind of helpless.

"So this is my dad," Peter said, looking into the casket. "Was," he corrected himself.

"I guess so," Hugh said, and hesitantly put his arm around Peter, not sure whether his brother needed solace or not.

"Huh," Peter said and shrugged. He looked over his shoulder at Hugh. "I'm not really sure what I thought would happen here. I guess I thought maybe I'd feel something. Thought maybe there'd be some kind of letting go."

"Not so much?" Hugh asked.

Peter shook his head. "It's just some guy's funeral. Some guy I didn't know."

They went out for beers after, to catch up. They talked about old times, about Pan and Pirates and the days before that first stint in juvie. They talked, too, about Albert Frank, about the fight, and about whether or not there had to be a first time. After both brothers were good and drunk, Hugh asked Peter something he had been wanting to know for years. That day in front of the mirror, had Peter known that nothing would happen, Hugh wondered. Had he believed the story himself, or had he been trying to teach Hugh a lesson?

Peter didn't know, he said, what Hugh was talking about. Had no memory of the day in question. Pirates and mirrors?

Must have just been some game they were playing. Must have just been a joke.

Hugh nodded and smiled, laughed and swigged his beer. Changed the subject and pretended to believe Peter, that it had all just been a game. That it had never meant anything at all.

WHEN I WAS TWELVE

When I was eleven and my dad disappeared, it didn't really affect me the way my mom expected it to. She called me into her room with this serious, stern look on her face, but then she kind of danced around it. Told me that she wanted me to know that what happened between her and my dad had nothing to do with me or Mike. That sometimes mommies and daddies just don't want to be together anymore.

I must have been experiencing those early warning signs of teen angst because I shrugged and said something like, "We're better off without him, anyway." Which was how I felt, but even at eleven I knew you weren't supposed to say things like that.

It was almost a full year later when she announced that my dad had gotten in touch with her, that she was flying down to Phoenix to meet him, and that she was sure that what he wanted to talk about was a divorce. I think she still thought we were going to react in some melodramatic way, like this was "a very special episode" of our lives. "I want you to know," she said, "that I'm here if you have any questions or if you just need to talk."

Mike and I kind of exchanged a look, which was momentous in and of itself, because Mike was five years older than me and seemed to think that acting like a brother was beneath him. "Are you going to leave us some money?" was all Mike wanted to know.

"Of course," my mom said, and she sounded relieved. I don't know why because it seemed to me like a rude thing to be concerned about. It was obvious she expected us to be thinking about other things. About her relationship with my dad, I guess, and about how this was going to affect the family as a whole.

My mom handed Mike some twenties and he stood there and counted them out, like he was verifying that she had given him correct change, before he slipped them into his wallet. "Pleasure doing business with you," Mike said. "Tell old Tom I said hi."

"Don't call your dad old Tom," my mom said.

"Do I have to watch Angela or what?"

They both looked at me like I couldn't speak English or something.

"I can watch myself," I said.

My mom turned back to Mike and said, "I'll pay you a little bit for babysitting."

"My rate's $25 a day."

"Your rate's what I say it is," my mom said.

"Alright, but you get what you pay for," Mike said.

"Michael. Enough."

Mike shook his head. "Are we done here? Because I have a date."

My mom sighed. "Alright, but be back early."

"I'll be back by midnight."

"By ten," my mom said. "I have to get to bed early. I'm leaving first thing in the morning."

"Fine," Mike said and left.

My mom turned to me and put her hands on my shoulders. "Angie, are you sure you're okay with this?"

"I'd rather just take care of myself," I said.

"No, sweetheart, I mean . . . you know, with what's happening. With me and your dad."

"It's none of my business," I said.

She tilted her head and scrunched her eyebrows together. "Well, sweetheart, it is your business. I mean, it isn't your fault, but you have a right to know what's going on."

"I know it's not my fault," I said. "Why would it be my fault?"

My mom nodded really slowly. "That's . . . right," she said. "Yes. That's right."

"I mean obviously it's Dad's fault. 'Cause he's an asshole."

"Angie!"

"I'm just saying, Mom. I mean, I don't care. It doesn't affect me. But, come on, he really is."

"Angie, honey, you don't have to feel that way just because of what he did to me."

"It's not that," I said, but I didn't go on.

The thing was I had never really had much of a relationship with my dad. It was like he had tested it out, gone for a trial run with Mike, but by the time I was born he had already gotten bored with the whole thing. The only real fatherly thing I can remember him ever doing was when I was six and he built me a tree house in the backyard. Although calling it a tree house was a stretch. Just a rickety plank that he had nailed into a big oak tree. But he sure made a big deal out of that plank. So proud of himself for doing something that fathers, as a rule, are supposed to do.

He had come home from work that day and called me out to the backyard, pointed at the tree and said, "I'm going to make you a tree house, sweetheart. What do you think about that?" I grabbed my favorite doll—Miss Mitsy—and a cup of juice and sat down on the cool grass to watch while he meticulously

41

got out his tools, took measurements of the trunk and the branches and the wood planks he had bought as remnants at the lumber yard, and then hammered a big plank into place on four branches. He tested its sturdiness by pressing down with the palm of his hand, and I watched in horror as it dipped down and then sprang back up again when he let go. He nodded, sliced his hands together to dust them off, and turned to me with a smile. He told me it wouldn't hold much weight and that I could only use it until I was ten, but I stopped climbing up there long before that.

But I didn't cite the tree house incident, or anything else, to my mom to explain why I wasn't upset about my dad being gone. I just shrugged and said again, "We're better off without him." My mom was probably kind of glad that I was on her side about the whole thing, but you could tell that she was trying to hide it. She sighed and squeezed my shoulders and then said, "Come on. Let's make dinner."

The next day after my mom left town, after my friend Lizzy insisted on spending the night, and after Mike used all the money my mom had given him, along with his fake ID, to buy cases and cases of cheap beer for an impromptu party, Lizzy and I ventured out of my bedroom and into Mike's party on a dare. We waded through the high school kids and puffs of marijuana smoke weighing down the air until we came to a guy sitting by himself in the corner of my living room, leaning against the wall with piles of crumpled beer cans surrounding him in a semicircle. Lizzy pointed and said, "That's the one. Him."

He was unbelievably ugly. I mean ugly. Repulsively, hideously unattractive. He had shaggy hair that wasn't dark enough to be brown, but wasn't light enough to be blond and so instead just looked sort of dirty and yet bland at the same time. His pockmarked face was bright red with the formation of fresh pimples; you could actually see new acne scars forming on top of the old ones, and they mingled together to make him look like he had lived a really hard life. He looked old, in his twenties at least. Much older than Mike and way too old for me.

I took one look at him and turned back to Lizzy, shaking my head. "No way," I said. "Nuh-uh."

"You have to, Angie," Lizzy said and nudged me with her elbow. "You can't just back out on a dare."

"You said I had to kiss someone. You didn't say you get to pick who," I said.

Lizzy looked the guy up and down, shook her head and turned back to me. "Come on, it's more fun this way," she said. "Besides, he's totally lonely. Look at him, all by himself. He'll be more open to it that way."

"What was the point of putting on makeup if we're just going to throw ourselves at the ugliest guy in the room?" I pawed at my eyes, which I'm sure smudged the blue and green eye shadow that Lizzy had liberally applied there.

We were both coated in makeup, had taken turns slathering it on each other after we broke into my mom's makeup drawer, which was a double crime, really, because it meant breaking my mom's rule that I wasn't allowed to wear makeup until I was sixteen. It had felt good, though, waiting expectantly as Lizzy applied and inspected and then applied some more, my mind racing with images of myself in makeup and long straight hair, like the women on TV. High heels and a miniskirt, too. I pictured myself walking into school carrying not a backpack but a purse, and all the girls and boys would turn and whisper to each other, "Didn't that used to be Angie Calhoun?" When I finally got to look in the mirror after Lizzy was done I saw my face transformed into a woman's, and that was where the idea of heading out to the party came from. The dare was just an excuse. The real point was that we looked beautiful and we wanted to be seen.

Lizzy shoved me in the direction of the ugly guy. "Come on," she said.

We walked over to him, and Lizzy put her arms on my shoulders and pressed down, forcing me to sit next to him. "Hi," she said to the guy. "My name's Lizzy. And this is Angie."

He looked at me and nodded, his eyes glazed over and dull. "Hi," he said into his beer can.

Lizzy sat down on the guy's other side. "Is that all you have to say?" she said. "Two pretty girls come up to you and you can't even give us your name?"

His brow knitted together, and he looked at Lizzy and then me. "How old are you guys?" he finally said.

Lizzy let out an elaborate fake laugh. "What, you don't think we're old enough to be here? This is Angie's party." She pointed at me.

He looked at me, head cocked to the side. "I thought this was Mike Calhoun's party."

"Mike's throwing it, but it's in honor of Angie," Lizzy said.

"Oh," the guy said and took a swig of his beer. "And how old are you again?"

I looked uncertainly at Lizzy, who said, "We're sixteen."

"Yeah," I said. "Sixteen."

"Fuck it," the guy said, took a long gulp of beer, then shook the empty can. "Doesn't matter, anyway. You ladies want some beer?" He reached over me to a mostly empty 24-pack of beer.

"Definitely," Lizzy said.

The guy handed me and Lizzy each a beer, then grabbed another for himself. "So are you, like, Mike's girlfriend or something?"

I wrinkled up my nose and stuck out my tongue but I could tell this was the wrong reaction when Lizzy's face folded in on itself in horror.

"Ex," Lizzy said quickly. "But he obviously still likes her." She swooped her arms around my crowded living room.

"Didn't work, though, eh?" the guy said, popping open a new beer and chugging what seemed like half the can in one go.

"Huh?" I asked.

He lowered the beer can from his mouth and then wiped away the foam dribbling down his chin with a quick swipe of the back of his forearm. "He's trying to get you back, right?"

"Oh," I said, and peered around the room looking for Mike. There were people dancing and people sitting on our couch— just really piled on top of each other's laps, making out—and there were people throwing things in each other's mouths and people pouring beer on each other's heads. But I didn't see my brother anywhere. I looked back at the guy. Lizzy had scooted over to him and she was whispering something in his ear.

He leaned in closer to her, a grin widening on his face. When she finished, his eyes flashed in my direction and he said, "Well, then. Well."

I looked at Lizzy and she smiled at me, leaning her back against the wall and gulping her beer.

"What do you say?" Lizzy asked the guy.

He nodded at me. "I'm game if you are."

I looked at Lizzy. "I'm not sure I . . ."

Lizzy laughed.

The guy looked at her, his teeth showing through his wide open grin. He looked like an animal flashing his fangs. "You wanted to make Mike jealous, right?"

"Oh," I said and blushed. "Yeah."

The guy scooted a little closer to me, put his arms around me, leaned in and breathed on me. He stank of beer and BO. "I think I can help you with that."

His mouth enveloped mine. It was much bigger than my own, so his lips were sort of encasing mine, not touching them but surrounding them. He was slurping and slobbering, and my entire face, it felt like, was getting all wet and sticky. His face pressed hard against mine, his teeth clacking against my teeth, and his tongue probed inside my mouth, reaching so far inside I thought I would gag.

I looked past the guy's head to Lizzy, who leaned up close to watch us, her eyes attentive. She craned her neck, the better to see where our mouths met and where our bodies pressed together.

His hands began to roam around my neck, and then down, and then further down and further still. It was rough and searching and when he stuck his hand inside my pants and started feeling around inside, it didn't feel the way it felt when I would do it, pretending that my hand was someone else's. It was fumbling and forceful, too much pressure and not in the right places.

Out of the corner of my eye, I saw Mike walk into the room from outside, his arm wrapped around some skinny blond girl with makeup that looked like it was melting. She was sort of leaning against him and he was almost dragging her along, she was so drunk and drooping. Her eyes half closed, she looked kind of dazed as she stumbled along beside my brother.

I closed my eyes and let the guy push my body onto the floor and press his weight on top of me. His erection—having never felt one before I could only assume that must be what it was—stabbed my leg, and his body was crushing mine. But I just lay there and let him move and pulse and grind on top of me. None of it mattered, anyway. I knew as soon as Mike saw us, he would break it apart and banish me and Lizzy to my room.

The guy pulled back, his weight lifted off of me a bit from the top, and I opened my eyes and saw that he was looking at Lizzy as she pressed something into his hand. She said something to him but I couldn't hear what because my ears were pounding. I could hear my heartbeat, loud and pulsing, and everything else was just background noise.

I couldn't see what Lizzy had given the guy but I knew what it was, all the same. My stomach had kind of somersaulted earlier that night when Lizzy had started to rummage through my sock drawer. Suddenly whatever we had been talking about— complaining, I think, about how loud Mike and his friends were being—had just sort of melted away. The only thing I could think about was that she was going to find it, and then she would know what a pervert I was.

Lizzy was older than me, a whole grade higher, but still, I wasn't completely sure she would even know what it was. She might think it was a piece of hard candy or something and just ignore it altogether. She claimed she wasn't a virgin, had slept with her third cousin or something like that, but I wasn't sure whether I believed her. When Lizzy found it, she said, "Ha!" like she had just caught me in a lie. She tossed it on the floor in front of me and said, "Looks like there's more to Angie than meets the eye."

"Oh, that," I said, trying to sound nonchalant. "I found it."

Lizzy picked it back up and carried it to my bed, lay down on her back, and held it in the air above her. "This is a good brand. Where did you find it?"

I shrugged. "I don't know. Just on the floor. What difference does it make? I just thought it might come in handy, that's all." I stood up and walked to the bed, sat down next to Lizzy.

Lizzy sat up and handed the condom to me. "You never know with these things. Gotta be prepared," she said.

I placed the condom face up in the palm of my hand and then closed my fingers around it. "I just figured sooner or later I would need one, so I might as well hang on to it."

"Sooner than later," Lizzy said. "You're almost a teenager. You gotta start acting your age."

"Yeah," I said, opening my fingers again and then closing them. "That's what I was thinking."

And I was thinking it again now, the same thing I had been thinking more and more lately. That I wasn't a little kid anymore. That I was ready. I looked back out across the living room, where Mike and the blond had been moments ago. But they weren't there anymore. I looked up again and the guy was staring down at me, holding the condom between his thumb and forefinger. "You wanna go find a room?" he asked.

I looked at Lizzy, who was nodding and smiling.

"Okay," I said.

He climbed off of me and then reached his hand down to pull me to my feet. The room spun around me as I stood up, and I felt wobbly.

"Come on," the guy said. He turned and started walking unsteadily toward the hallway.

Lizzy nudged me from behind. "You're welcome," I heard her say.

I looked back at her, then turned and watched the guy stumble down the hallway. He knocked and opened Mike's door, then closed it, then knocked on my mom's door, opened it, and looked back at me and nodded before he disappeared inside.

I started to walk toward the hallway, tried to make my way through the ocean of people that filled my living room, but it was like I was caught in the current. There were people everywhere and they were swirling in different directions around me and they were jostling and bumping me toward the hallway.

And then I spun around and bolted for the back door.

I felt Lizzy's fingers graze my shirt but I shot away from her, scurrying outside and up to my tree house. As I stepped onto the thin plank of wood I felt it shift, bend under my weight, and I braced myself for the fall. But then the plank steadied, and I sat down and scooted back out of the line of sight of anyone from the ground. Not that anyone was looking up at me. I wrapped my arms around my knees, turning them into a cradle, and dropped my head into them. I could feel the branches shifting beneath me in the breeze. I knew this was dangerous, knew the plank was probably straining beneath my weight, but I decided to wait out the night there, anyway, listening to the branches creak and wondering if the plank would hold.

Or maybe that isn't what happened at all. Maybe that's just how I prefer to remember it. Because it's better than remembering the long, slow march down the hallway to my mom's room, then watching as the ugly guy closed the door behind me, stripped off his clothes to reveal his acne inflamed body, his thick, hard penis, the first I had ever seen. I would later realize it was much larger than most, an unhappy twist of fate that probably doesn't matter but feels like it should.

And I don't like thinking about how I took my clothes off, too, how I climbed onto my mom's pink and purple wedding quilt—the quilt my dad had never liked because pink and purple, he said, were girl colors. How I cringed as the ugly guy climbed on top of me, spread my legs apart and then paused to open the condom package with his teeth and roll it on. Then he jabbed and jabbed and jabbed me with his penis until he finally broke through. Or how I bled and cried. Or how after he was finished, he climbed off of me, threw his clothes back on, and left without a word, leaving the door standing open behind him.

49

I just lay there for a minute, naked in a puddle of murky blood, and waited for something to happen, for someone to come in and find me and scold me for being bad. But nobody did.

When I put my clothes back on and walked back into my bedroom, Lizzy was still in the living room, at the party. I climbed into my bed, closed my eyes, and went to sleep.

The next morning, after Lizzy went home, I threw my mom's quilt in the washer and took an hour long shower. When my mom got home later, she came straight into my room, sat down on the side of my bed, where I had been lying on top of the covers staring at the ceiling, and set her suitcase down on my floor. She told me she needed to talk to me about something pretty important and I figured she was worried about breaking the news about the divorce, like I didn't already know that she and my dad were going to get a divorce. Like it would change anything anyway.

"Well I met with your dad yesterday," she said and then paused, sighed, brushed the hair off of my forehead.

"I know," I said.

"Don't you want to know what we talked about?" she asked.

I sat up, rubbed my eyes, and shrugged. "I think I can guess."

"Really?" She looked startled. "Well, how do you feel about it?"

I shrugged again. "I don't really care."

She nodded. "Well, I have to admit, I have my reservations. Your dad caused a lot of pain when he left."

I nodded.

"But I just don't know if I can do this by myself," she said.

I nodded again, but a little more slowly. I wasn't sure anymore what she was talking about.

"We're just going to try it," she said. "A trial unseparation, you could say."

"Dad's moving back in with us?" I asked.

"We're just going to try it," she said again. "He's flying in later today."

When my dad arrived a few hours later, my mom called me into the living room to greet him. My dad just stood in the doorway, a suitcase in each hand, like he couldn't come any further until someone invited him in. My mom nodded at him and apparently that was enough because he walked up to me, put down his luggage, and told me how much he had missed me.

He told me how sorry he was that he hadn't been there for my last birthday but that I should know that he had been thinking of me on my special day. And then he pulled out of one of his suitcases a little unwrapped jewelry box with my name engraved in gold on the side. Only it wasn't really my name, the name I actually went by: Angie. It was the name that was printed on my birth certificate: Angela. A common enough name. A name you could easily find printed on the "personalized" knickknacks for sale in an airport gift shop.

He held the jewelry box out to me like it was some kind of precious jewel, a family heirloom or something, and his eyes gleamed as he told me to "Open it."

I pulled the lid open and a little ballerina in a pink tutu— pink, a girl's color, my dad believed—jumped up on a spring and began to dance and twirl as a tinny tune played. "Oh," I said.

"What do you think?" he asked me, bending his knees and resting his hands on his thighs. "Do you like it?"

I fought the urge to tell him that I had never liked pink or ballet and I was way too old for that sort of thing. "Neat," I said and closed the lid.

51

"What do you say?" my mom asked.

"Thank you."

"You're welcome, sweetheart," my dad said, standing up again and ruffling my hair.

That night when my mom came into my room to kiss me goodnight, she told me how mature she thought I was being for not pointing out how inappropriate the gift had been and how little my own dad knew me. "You're being very grown-up," she told me. "I'm proud of you. You've turned into such a woman."

I didn't tell her that I had smashed the jewelry box the second I was left alone in my room, or that I had silently resolved that I hated my dad and would hate him forever. I didn't tell her anything, just kissed her on the cheek and said goodnight and then lay awake all night long, wondering if it really was true. If I was a woman now.

THE KIND THAT CAN BE REAL

1

Michael doesn't seem to think I'm strange, a small and simple thing that means a lot, if you really think about it, especially since Burt didn't even try to mask his uncertainty about hiring a thirty-year-old woman who has never worked a day in her life. But Burt trusts the agency, he said, and he's never been one to jump to conclusions unwarranted.

"I pledge to you, sir, that I will not disappoint you," I told Burt when he offered me the job. This was after, of course, I had clapped my hands together and jumped up and down in excitement several times.

He just shook his head and said, "See, this is what I'm talking about. Nobody in the world talks the way you talk."

I don't know what Burt finds so off-putting about the way that I speak, but everything I say he seems to think outrageous. Michael, though, doesn't knit his brows together when I introduce myself to him, doesn't tilt his head to the side and inspect me like I'm some kind of anomaly, and I feel relieved that it will be Michael, and not Burt, who will be training me.

Michael is short and sort of soggy in the middle, but his blue eyes redeem his looks. They're that kind of blue, dark and unfathomable, that's almost periwinkle but not quite. Almost purple. But other than that, there is nothing really different about him, nothing to set him apart from the others in the office, who are all dressed in similar clothes and subdued colors and who don't any of them look anything like me. There is nothing different about Michael except that his shirt is wrinkled a little bit at the hem of his right sleeve. It feels important, this small distinction, the difference between trying to be and actually being unique.

"It's very nice to meet you," I say and take Michael's hand, squeeze it affectionately. I'm trying to let him know how much I appreciate the wrinkles on his sleeve. Spider webs of red creep up Michael's neck and then spread across his face and up his forehead like a fire. His hand goes limp in mine, so I let it go. I like him immediately because even though he looks mostly like the others, even though his slacks are grey and his button up shirt is a plain and empty white, he doesn't seem to notice that I don't look like the rest or that there is a tuft of black hair poking out from the top of my canvas bag. Or at least, if he notices, he doesn't seem to care.

As Michael leads me out of the conference room and down the cubicle corridor, I feel like I am being watched by everybody in the office, even though when I try to catch them looking, they all glance away. A woman with bobby pins placed seemingly at random throughout her loose bun does look up, though, and she nods at me when Michael and I walk past her. I stop, lift the hem of my white cotton dress and pink pinafore layered on top of it, and I curtsey. She looks back down at her computer.

Michael looks back and pauses his stride, lets me catch up with him. Then he leans in to me and says, "May want to get some more work appropriate attire," in a lowered voice. "Burt can be an ass about these things."

I look down at my pinafore, at my white cotton socks trimmed with lace, my low heeled Mary Janes, and then back up at the people in the office. The colors of their clothes sort of run into each other to make the entire office a dull and muddy brown, like what happens with my finger paints when I go overboard, try too hard.

I shrug at Michael. "I was wondering why Burt was looking at me like that. I thought maybe it was my hair. I still haven't gotten the hang of doing it myself." I pull my loose pigtails over my shoulders and smooth my fingers across the flyaway strands.

Michael glances at the braids but doesn't say anything. Keeps leading me to the cubicle we will share, where he will teach me everything I need to know about insurance claims and medical coding. When we get there, he motions at the empty desk that I assume is mine and says, "I'll just give you a second to get situated."

I turn and look at the long rectangular desktop, blank but for a computer. I turn back to Michael, not sure what he expects me to do. He's already sitting down at his desk with his back to me, rustling papers and typing intermittently.

His desk is scattered with papers and office supplies. Loose pens, a stapler, a random distribution of different sized paper clips. Lined up in neat succession along the wall is a series of little plastic men. Men in capes. Men with masks. Men with hard, flexed muscles and carefully painted grimaces.

I stare at them for a second, look from the men to Michael, who looks nothing like any of them, and back to the men. Some of them are squatting, some hold guns or grenades. One has a quiver strapped to his back. For a second, I wonder if these are the right kind, like Mindy, but as I take in their stiff plastic bodies, their painted facial expressions and clothes, I know that they aren't. Either they're not the right type or Michael isn't, but

55

either way, they're nothing more than toys, these men, and I can tell toys are all they'll ever be.

I reach into my shoulder bag and pull out Mindy. After I prop her up on the desk beside the computer, I drop my now empty bag on the floor and kick it under my desk. I sit down and say, "Okay. I'm situated."

Michael swivels his chair around and looks at Mindy's shiny purple eyes, the smudged plastic on her face, her hands, her legs, and her long black hair which is beginning to mat a little with age. He laughs but not in a mean way.

"Michael, I'd like you to meet Mindy. Mindy, this is Michael."

I pull her string and she says, "My name's Mindy, and I love you."

Michael laughs again and stands up, steps to my desk and reaches his hand out to shake Mindy's. "Pleasure to meet you." He looks me in the eyes. The red spider webs cross his neck again, and he turns away. He points to the little men stationed at the back of his desk and says, "These are my ones," and he doesn't look at me as he says it.

"Yeah, I saw them. Who are they?" I roll my chair over and pick up one of the guys, a man with huge muscles and red hair that spirals off the top of his head.

"Just different action figures from when I was a kid," he says. "That's the Fickle Fire."

"The Fickle Fire?" I ask.

"You don't remember the Fickle Fire? I used to watch it every Saturday morning."

"I never had a TV. My Grammie said it's bad for your mind." I pump the man's little plastic arms up and down and inspect his chipped body, his tiny removable laser gun. "Wow," I say. "This is so cool." I squeeze the gun between my thumb and index finger and point it at Michael. Pretending to shoot at him, I say, "P-pew, pew."

Michael is supposed to grab his chest, through which the laser has quite thoroughly burned a hole, but he doesn't. He just laughs and says, "Yeah. You gotta have something to get you through the days of slogging through CPT and ICD9 codes."

"CPT and ICD9? What's that?" I ask, putting the gun back in the little man's hand.

Michael reaches out and takes the Fickle Fire from me, places him gingerly back on the desk. "I guess that's my cue to start training you," he says. "Let's get down to business."

I take a pining look at the men, wondering whether we'll get a chance to play during our breaks. "If we have to," I say. "If we really have to."

2

Mindy doesn't like the plastic men. Doesn't like to think about them standing there side by side on Michael's desk, muscles flexed and permanent scowls on their faces. She tells me so over tea, both of us sitting at my red wooden table, which has three matching chairs that have hearts carved into their backs. Grammie gave me this table when I was little, but I still use it because I love it. I don't care that it's small, is made for children's bodies, children's short, spindly legs. It's sturdy enough.

Mindy watches me blow away the steam rising from my old, partially melted plastic teacup. "They look mean," she says. "And it's no wonder. Michael just left them there when he went home for the day."

I take a sip of tea and say nothing.

Mindy motions for me to pull her string again and I do. "He's the sort of person Grammie warned you about, Rhetta. The sort you have to be careful of."

"I know," I say. "But Grammie isn't here." I feel guilty for saying it, but I can't take it back.

Mindy nods, and I pull her string again. "Just be careful. Dolls reflect their owners," she says. "And those dolls are mean."

Dolls reflect their owners: it's something Mindy taught me a long time ago. Because Mama had a doll, too. We found her buried in a pile of shoes in Mama's walk-in closet. Mama slept during the day because she danced at night, and sometimes Mindy and I would quietly sneak into her room to borrow books or to play dress up or to play with Mama's body glitter.

One time, Mindy and I were in Mama's closet looking for some shoes to play dress up with. Mama's heels were all too high and sharp, so we kept digging deeper and deeper, hoping to find something that might work. And there she was: the doll. She had blond hair, like mine, like Mama's, and little blue eyes that stared straight ahead. She was naked for some reason, her little plastic body dirty from the shoes, and she smelled like leather and vanilla-scented shoe inserts.

I pulled her out of the shoes and looked at her, moved my hands up and around, but her eyes didn't follow my movement. "Hello?" I whispered. Mama was asleep on her bed and I didn't want to wake her. "My name's Rhetta and this is Mindy."

Mindy drew back a little and looked up at me.

The blond doll didn't move.

"Mindy," I whispered. "Is she the right kind?"

Mindy stepped over to the doll cautiously and leaned down to inspect her more closely. She looked back at me and nodded slowly, but the expression on her face was grim.

"Hi," I whispered again to the doll. "We're nice, I promise. You can talk to us."

But the doll didn't move.

Mindy looked up and shook her head at me.

Later Mindy would explain it to me, that dolls reflect their owners. She said that because she was my doll, she was good. But Mama's doll would be bad because Mama was a bad person. Mama was mean and Mama did bad things like say curse words and let men see her naked. Mama yelled a lot, too. So Mama's doll, Mindy said, must be very bad news.

"You can see it in her eyes," Mindy told me. "There's something not right about them."

"They're blue," I said, because I didn't know what else she meant. "They look just like Mama's eyes."

"But not just the color," Mindy said. "It's something more. It's like they're empty. It's like there's nothing behind them at all."

"Maybe she isn't the kind after all," I said.

But Mindy shook her head. I pulled her string again but all she said was, "She is," and then static filled the air as the string slithered the rest of the way back inside its hole.

3

In spite of Michael's angry little men, who I'm beginning to realize we will never have time to play with, I like this job. I've read about jobs like this, office jobs with cubicles and endless typing. They're always depicted as being gloomy and boring and unapologetically meaningless, but this job is nothing like that.

For one thing, it feels like it matters. Like we're helping people. I think about that when Michael lets me tackle my first pile of claims on my own. How good it feels to be doing something. To be given a chance to make a difference in the world.

I shift Mindy forward so that she is slumped over and her head tilts down. This way she can see each claim as I flatten it on the desk in front of me and glance through its visit notes, match its CPT codes to its ICD9s.

I'm supposed to figure out whether we should pay for each claim. It's as simple as scanning through the information, pulling up the patient's policy, and making sure that whatever the doctor did is covered. These claims are being billed to us because the doctor's offices have already determined that we should pay them, so it only takes a few seconds to scan through the details and stamp each claim with my "Accept" stamp. My "Deny" stamp, which I've used so far only twice, is big and bulky. It has a huge space underneath the crisp letters for me to write in the reason for the denial.

I'm almost surprised at how easy the job is. How simple having a job would have been all along. I glance at Mindy and she smiles quickly at me then straightens her expression again so no one will see. I was so afraid of what it would be like, working. Every book I've ever read that deals with work at all deals with it like it's this miserable thing, like it sucks all the fun out of life. But this is its own kind of fun.

I begin to hum softly to myself this tune that Grammie used to sing sometimes, and bob my head from side to side as I scan through each claim, check it against the database, and then stamp it firmly and move it to the pile of acceptances on my right.

After a while, a dark shadow casts itself over my desk. I look up, see Burt hovering behind me.

He clears his throat. "Just figured I should check on how you're doing. Getting the hang of it okay?"

I nod. "Yep. Look how many I've already gotten through." I point to my acceptance pile and feel proud at how tall it is, how imposing.

He nods. "Did Michael tell you you're supposed to separate the accepted claims from the denied ones?"

Michael swivels his chair and rolls it over. "Yeah." He looks at my acceptance stack. "Didn't I?"

"Yeah," I say. "I'm separating them." I point to the small denied pile, two claims high, on the other side of the acceptances.

"Your acceptances?" Burt asks as he reaches down and picks one of my denials up, reads the angled stamp I pressed into it, and then looks back at me, his eyebrows raised.

Michael leans forward and lifts the top acceptance off the pile, registers its stamp, and then looks up at Burt.

"These are my acceptances." I point at the big pile, even though I know they've already figured that much out.

Burt places the claim he's holding on top of the other denied claim. As though I'm not even there, Burt stares at the acceptance pile and says, "Michael, can I see you in my office please?"

Red spider webs crawl up Michael's face and he nods. He's not looking at me either as he places his claim back where he got it. Michael stands, and he and Burt march away.

I can't help but blush too, in spite of myself, because I don't know what I did wrong, but it's obvious that I've gotten Michael in trouble. I look down at Mindy and am not surprised to see that she's almost imperceptibly blushing also.

I look at the denials, dwarfed by the acceptances beside them, and feel overwhelmed by panic. I don't know what I'm doing. Why did I think that I did? I shouldn't be here. This is what Mama used to talk about: the ways of the world and reality and all that.

I stand up and rush to the bathroom, lock myself in a stall, and try to stifle the sound of my sobs. I just keep thinking over and over that I'm not capable. Not qualified. I don't know what I'm doing, and I can't. I can't. I can't.

4

Mindy is downing her tea tonight, but I'm just sitting here staring at my cup and the feather-light shortbread cookie I moved onto my plate more for Mindy's benefit than my own. I'm not in the mood for a cookie tonight, or tea, and I don't know how to ask Mindy to imagine up something different for us to eat—some of Grammie's meatloaf, maybe, or beef stew. Mindy always gives me what she thinks I want and it would break her heart to find out that she guessed wrong this time. And anyway, it isn't really the food that's bothering me. It's Michael and Burt and the denial and acceptance piles at work. By the time I left for the day, Michael still hadn't come back from Burt's office.

I pick up my teacup and cradle it in my hands, just so Mindy won't notice that I'm not drinking it. "Mindy, did you see that look Burt gave me?"

She lowers the cup to her chin and tilts then shakes her head.

"At the office?"

She shrugs and takes another sip of tea.

"I think I'm doing something wrong. I think I'm going to get in trouble."

Mindy looks up and motions for me to pull her string. When I do, "Don't be silly, Rhetta," is all she says.

I want to point out that she blushed, too. That I know that she knows that I did something wrong. But I'm uncomfortable enough with the idea of Michael being mad at me. I don't want Mindy to be mad at me, too. "I don't know," I say. "The way he looked at the pile . . . I did something wrong, I know it."

Mindy smiles. "Oh come on. You've got nothing to be worried about. Eat your cookie." Mindy waves at the cookie on my plate.

I pick my cookie up, dip it in the tea, then take a tiny nibble and drop it back onto the plate. "I'm not really hungry."

Mindy doesn't acknowledge this, just reaches forward and picks up another cookie.

"Mindy, that look. I've seen it before."

Her chewing slows, then stops, then starts back up again. She takes another sip of tea and avoids my gaze.

"Mindy," I say.

I pull her string. "Let's go to bed." She lifts her arms in the air for me to pick her up.

I scoot my chair out and lift Mindy into my arms. I carry her to the bed—my pink princess bed that Grammie special ordered to fit my size—and lay her down. She rolls over on her back and pretends to fall asleep just like that, but I know her too well. I know that she is faking.

But I play along, climb out of my clothes and into my nightie without saying anything, and then I switch off the light, pull the blanket back and climb underneath it beside Mindy. I wrap my arms around her and rest my head against hers, but I can't sleep yet. Can't get the picture out of my head: Burt's gaze locked on my acceptance pile. The same look in his eyes as the one in Mama's when she used to scold me.

The strongest I ever saw that look was the time I spilled the books all over Mama's floor. When Grammie came in and found us, Grammie had the look too, only it was directed at Mama. Grammie didn't know what Mama was mad about. I didn't want her to know because Grammie would be mad just like Mama was once she found out. Grammie didn't like me going through Mama's books to begin with. Said they weren't appropriate for a girl my age.

There was just something exciting about Mama's books. They were so different from the ones Grammie would give me and the ones she read aloud to me at night. Those ones were good, too, about magic and pets and adventures and just being a kid. But Mama's books were about things I had never experienced, things like romance and war. Misery. Pain. They were peopled with characters who couldn't quite figure life out, who found themselves, page after page, just trying the best they could to make it all mean something. Mama's books made me feel. The struggles these characters were dealing with, it felt like they mattered in a way that the stories about magic and pets and kids with photographic memories never could.

Usually I would pick a book off of Mama's bookshelf, sneak it back into my room, and read it hiding under the bed or in a fortress I had made out of pillows and sheets. But that day I had been particularly indecisive. I remember lifting a book off a shelf, glancing at its cover and title and then reading its description on the back, and then, not being quite sure yet, placing it on the floor next to Mindy in one of three piles: "Probably," "Maybe," and "Deserves a Second Glance." I had made a sizable contribution to each of the piles when Mama started shifting around in her bed. Before I could make a quick decision and put the rest away, I heard Grammie's voice calling to me from the kitchen. "Rhetta! Cookies!"

Mama must have heard it, too, because she stirred again, smacked her lips together, and I knew if she woke up just now she would assume it had been me that had awakened her.

A floorboard in the hall popped. "Rhetta?" Grammie's voice, a bit louder, just outside Mama's room.

Mama turned over on the bed. Moaned.

I grabbed the book off the top of the "Probably" pile. In my rush to scoop the rest of the books up and hurriedly replace them on their shelves, I toppled the three piles into each other, making a huge crashing sound and waking Mama the rest of the way up.

"Rhetta," she hissed.

I turned and looked at her, my arms full of books that were falling, one by one, down to the ground like a slow motion waterfall. "I'm sorry, Mama. I'm sorry," I said. Without really meaning to, I began to cry.

The door swung open and Grammie walked in. She stood there for a second just staring at me, tears running down my cheeks and exploding like little bombs on the covers of Mama's books. The books kept tumbling down, flapping through the air before landing half open on top of each other on the floor. Then Grammie turned to Mama, who was sitting up in bed with her arms folded. "What's going on? What did you do?"

Mama swung her legs out of bed. "I didn't do anything. She just startled me."

"She's in hysterics," Grammie said, stepping over to me and wrapping me in a hug.

I dropped the rest of the books when Grammie pulled me into her arms, which made me cry even harder. Mama's beautiful books, they were bending and tearing.

Mama walked over to us and pulled Grammie off of me. "She's too sensitive."

Grammie pressed me against her chest, shielding me from Mama, and cooed into my ear, "It's okay, sweetheart. Shh. Shh."

Mama let out an exasperated sigh. "Ma, please. I can handle this. Rhetta, you need to clean this mess up, now, alright? No more blubbering." She leaned down and picked one of the books off the ground and handed it to me.

I reached out to take it, but Grammie snatched it away. "Not now, Nancy. The poor thing is terrified."

I sniffled into Grammie's shoulder, tried to restrain my tears. "It's okay," I said.

Grammie pressed my face to her chest and said, "That's right, sweetheart. It's okay." She grabbed Mindy off the floor, scooped me into her arms, and carried us both out of the room, ignoring Mama's complaints.

Grammie gave me and Mindy some cookies and a glass of milk and then she sat and watched me eat, blotting at my cheeks with a napkin. When Mama emerged from her room she was dressed for the drive to work, in her pink sweat suit and white sneakers. She smacked the palm of her hand against the table and then pointed at Grammie. "You," she said slowly, pronouncing each word with precision, "are not her mother."

Grammie didn't say anything, just reached to the platter she had placed in the center of the table and handed me another cookie.

Mama turned to me. "No more cookies until you clean up the mess you made."

I looked at Grammie, then at the cookie in my hand, then at Mama.

Mama cocked her hip and raised her eyebrows, waiting for me to respond.

I slid my chair out and dropped off of it, grabbed Mindy and began to walk around the table to the hall.

Grammie caught my arm. "Rhetta, you can finish your milk and cookies first. Then you can clean up the books."

Mama balled her hands into fists, threw her head back and shrieked. "Stay out of this!"

Grammie didn't defend herself, but she didn't drop her hand from my arm, either.

I stood there frozen for a second, not sure what to do. I thought I might start to cry again. I looked down at my feet, willing them to go one way or the other. To walk down the hallway and clean up my mess, or to walk back to my seat and have another cookie. But my feet didn't move. Just stayed still and waited for me to decide.

"Rhetta, go. I'm not leaving until you go."

"Rhetta, sit down. I'll go do it. I could use the exercise anyway."

I looked down at Mindy. Her head was pointed at Grammie, like she didn't even want to acknowledge Mama at all.

Mama grabbed Mindy and lifted her out of my reach. "Fine. You're grounded from Mindy for a week."

"Mama!"

"Nancy, no." Grammie stood up.

"I'll do it," I said. "I'll do it right now. See?" I took off running down the hall and into Mama's room, where I started to rummage through the books, alphabetizing and arranging them. I didn't look up from my task, was too busy biting back the tears and trying to finish. Even so, I heard Grammie and Mama arguing out there, like always, and then after a bit, the front door slammed.

Out of the corner of my eye, I saw a figure appear in the doorway.

"I'm doing it," I said and choked on a sob welling up in my throat. I stopped and squeezed my eyes shut, tried to keep any more tears from sneaking out, and when I opened them again

Grammie was kneeling down beside me. She handed Mindy to me and then reached her hand out for mine. She led me back to the kitchen and fed me more milk and cookies and then, after I had almost forgotten the whole thing, she said, "I'll clean the books up, Rhetta, but you shouldn't be getting into your Mama's books, okay?"

She left me there with the cookies and with Mindy, and I sat and listened to her humming down in Mama's room as she cleaned up my mess.

5

When I get to the office my two imbalanced piles are gone and Michael has an abnormally large stack of claims on his desk. He glances up when I approach, pulls some of the claims into his hands and watches as I set Mindy on my desk and sit down. I know that he's waiting to say something, to tell me whatever Burt told him yesterday, but he just kind of sits there for a second, looking down and up, from the claims to me.

"Morning, Michael," I say.

"Morning, Rhetta," he says.

"Whatcha got there?"

His neck turns red but he forces it down before it rushes all the way up his face. "I think we've had a bit of a miscommunication somewhere along the line." He rolls his chair over to my desk and lays the claims in front of me on the table.

I pick the top one off. The "Accepted" stamp I marked on it yesterday has been Xed out in vivid red and beside it is a "Denied" stamp with a series of absurd excuses jotted into the open space. "The CPT doesn't match the ICD9? In what way?" I ask.

Michael sighs. "You have to understand, it's our job to deny as many claims as we can. I don't think I explained it to you right."

"I accepted too many claims." I'm saying it, really, to Mindy, who is sitting on my desk trying to pretend like she doesn't hear.

"It's not a bad thing. I mean, it is from Burt's perspective I guess. But everybody does it at first. You think when you start that you're supposed to accept or deny based on the coverage of the patient's policy."

"But isn't that what we're supposed to do?"

Michael leans back in his chair. "On the surface, sure. But anything that can conceivably be denied should be."

"Oh," I say, but I still don't get it.

He points at the list of excuses under the word Denied. "We're not really trying to determine whether or not a service is covered. It's more like we're looking for reasons to deny each claim," he says. "The doctor wrote a CPT code that doesn't quite match the ICD9. The patient has a pre-existing condition that could by some stretch of the imagination relate to whatever he was seen for." He doesn't bother with the rest of the list. Instead, he picks up another claim from the stack and glances at it. "The explanation on the visit notes isn't detailed enough. Which leg went numb, was it the right or the left?" He gives me the claim and picks up another.

"Oh," I say again, staring down at the claim in my hands.

"Sometimes they'll submit it again," he says, looking down at the new claim. "Sometimes we can still find reasons to deny it. The claims start to taper off and the doctors get tired of waiting and switch the patients to Self Pay."

"I see." I nod. "I get it."

"It just takes a while to get the hang of it," he says. "It's like a game where the object is, I don't know, to keep your job, I guess. And the rules are to find whatever excuse you can to deny as many claims as possible."

I nod again. "I think I understand now. I'm sorry if I got you in trouble with Burt."

Michael shrugs. "Totally my fault. I was responsible for training you and I obviously didn't do it right." He takes the two claims in my hands and puts them on top of the pile, lifts it up and rolls his chair back to his desk. He grabs another pile and hands it to me. "Ready to have another go?"

I smile. "Yes. And Michael?"

He looks into my eyes.

"Thanks for not being mad at me."

Red spider webs. He looks away. "Don't be ridiculous. You're new. It happens." He turns his chair around and recommences sifting through the claims on his desk.

Already it's like I'm not there to him. He picks up a claim, reads it carefully and then his eyes go unfocused for a second as he works out how to deny it. He looks like the little old men who used to sit at the park opposite each other playing dominoes on a foldout table, back when Grammie used to walk with me down to the park. One of the men had long, white hair that cascaded over his shoulders and down to the ground. The first time I saw him I thought he was a lady. The other man had no hair at all. Instead, he had spots all over his head, big brown spots that Grammie had to remind me every time not to stare at. Their eyes would go unfocused when they were planning out their next move, hands hovering over the table in anticipation.

I watch Michael stamp the claim and scribble something quickly in the open space. It's a game. A puzzle. A challenge.

I plunge into the mound of claims in front of me. I work my way through them, denying as many as I can, which now that I'm starting to understand the way it works is most of them. I deny a claim because the photocopied visit notes are scrawled in what I claim to be illegible handwriting, though the slanted loops and open blotches look a lot like my own handwriting, so I can decode them easily enough. I deny another claim because a patient's knee gave out, but he has diabetes as an uncovered pre-existing condition, so I say that the knee may be linked to weight—the patient is pushing two hundred pounds—which may be linked to diabetes.

There's only one claim that really stumps me, but it stumps me hard. This patient has been suffering from increasingly frequent bouts of vertigo and has taken to passing out unexpectedly during the day. He's fairly healthy otherwise, and the lab tests show nothing out of the ordinary. The doctor wants him to go for some imaging. Thinks there's probably a neurological problem to blame.

But it's going to cost. A lot. If we approve this visit, there will be another much bigger bill to follow soon. And if they find anything wrong with the patient's nervous system, there will be another bill and another and another. If there was ever a claim I was meant to deny, it's this one. Yet there's an urgency to the visit notes. The doctor thinks the patient needs help and fast. If I deny his claim, even if just to tie it up in the system for a while, the patient's problem might get worse. He might die, for all I know.

"Michael?" I say and roll my chair over to his desk.

"What's up?"

"I need help with this one." I lay the claim on the desk in front of him.

He picks it up and scans through it. Frowns. Shakes his head. "If you accept this, Burt is going to lose it." He hands the claim back to me.

"I don't think Burt likes me," I say.

Michael snorts. "I don't think Burt likes anyone."

"What should I do?"

"I don't know." He looks at me, holds my gaze for a few seconds. I wait for the red spider webs to crawl up his neck, but they don't. "He might fire you, Rhetta."

"I need this job," I say, glancing back at Mindy on my desk.

Michael nods. "I guess you have to decide what's more important."

"What would you do?" I ask.

He looks back down at the claim like it's infected. "I'd deny it and tell Burt to go to hell."

"Really?"

His eyes roam back up to mine and then the red appears. He turns his eyes to the wall. "No." He shakes his head. Laughs a fake sort of dark and angry laugh, strangled, like what he really wants to do is cry. "This job is so fucked up sometimes."

My face goes hot when he says that word. Grammie told me once that only bad people use that word, but Michael doesn't seem bad, and he doesn't seem embarrassed either. It's a symbol, though, for the bad thing. The thing Grammie said don't ever do, and I never did. I wonder, briefly, if Michael has ever done it, but I push the thought away.

I roll back over to my desk and lay the claim flat in front of me. I stare down at the patient's name, Trent McMann, and wonder what he's like. Whether or not he's poor. Whether he will go and get the imaging done anyway or whether he'll just keep on passing out until whatever is wrong inside his brain finally shuts him down altogether, or maybe until he passes out somewhere dangerous and hits his head on something sharp.

I look into Mindy's purple eyes, which have shifted to mine and stare at me pleadingly. I don't want to let Trent McMann down, but I can't let Mindy down. Mindy's eyes pull me in. She's trying to talk to me, trying to tell me something. I stare intently into the purple and realize that I can hear her in my head, as though I had pulled her string. Things always work out in the end, she wants me to know. Even if his claim is denied, he'll be okay. He probably has people in his life that love him, people with good jobs that can afford to take care of him. He probably even has a wife. Yes, that's it. A young, beautiful wife who will stay by his side the entire time, who will love him and cherish him and nurse him back to health, and their marriage will be stronger because of it.

I bring the stamp down on the claim and scribble quickly in the open space. "Not enough information. Need a second opinion."

I add it to my denied pile, and then I glance back at Michael, see that he's watching me. The red spider webs make their way up his face and he turns back around to his desk, looking down.

6

Tonight as we drink our tea, Mindy gushes. "I'm so proud of you," she says. "You're doing so well. You'll probably get promoted before you know it."

I let her talk, pull her string and pull it again, let her keep going and going while I sit quietly and sip my tea, which tastes bland tonight. I don't know why. I'm only really half listening to Mindy at all, half taking in her enthusiasm. The other half

73

of my mind is trying to reconcile things: Mindy and my job, Michael and the denials. Michael doesn't seem to believe in what we have to do, but he does it anyway. I'm not sure what to make of that.

But Mama told me once that, more than anything, life is about doing what has to be done. The sooner you realize that, the better. She went out of her way to teach me about the real world, like the night she came into my room and woke me up. It was late, I know that, but I don't know how late. I was only seven and Grammie was still in the habit of sending me to bed pretty much right after dinner. All I know is that the world around me was dark, and I was asleep already, Mindy cradled in my arms, when Mama threw my door open with a loud bang and stumbled into my room.

The thump of the door slamming against my wall woke me up, but I kept my eyes pressed shut because I didn't know if it was a monster or my Mama, and I didn't know if it made much difference, either way. I lay there shivering with Mindy in my arms and listened as my Mama made her slow, clumsy way over to my bed.

She stood over me for a moment, sipping the air in shallow breaths, and I just kept hugging Mindy tighter and tighter, hoping that Mama would just go away. But she didn't. She sat down on the side of my bed and pressed her fingertips into my cheek. "Hey," she said in a drawling voice. "Hey, Rhe-tta." She pronounced each syllable carefully and poked my cheek a little harder with each one.

I peeled my eyes open, trying to pretend like I was just waking up, and rubbed them with one hand, keeping my other arm wrapped around Mindy. "Mama?" She smelled like my Mama, that stale smell that Grammie said came from the club, and she sounded like my Mama, or at least, the way my Mama sounded sometimes when she was tired or angry. But in the dark, she was just a looming figure, a shadow sitting on my bed and staring down at me, her face only barely illuminated by the moonlight shining in through my window.

"Did I wake you?" she asked.

The warmth of her breath beat down on my face and I thought it might stifle me. I had to force myself not to pull back. "Uh-huh." I nodded.

She didn't say anything for a second, just sat on the edge of my bed and watched me, her head tilted to one side. The whites of her eyes, which seemed almost to glow in the dim light, flicked up and down and from this side to that. For a second her eyes lingered on Mindy, and I instinctively squeezed Mindy a little closer to me.

"Mama?" I asked. "Is everything okay?"

Mama looked into my eyes so long and so hard it was like she was trying to remember who I was. Finally, she shook her head and said, "You don't understand, Rhetta. I have to make you understand."

I glanced at the door, wondering if Grammie was still awake. "Understand what, Mama?"

Mama shook her head again and started to laugh. "Exactly," she said. "See what I mean?" She leaned over to my bedside table and switched on my ballerina lamp.

The light made everything clear so suddenly I couldn't stop myself—I shrank back, pressing my little body hard into the mattress. Mama's face was all distorted, puffy and discolored in shades of pink and purple and blue. Brown tapering into black. The skin around her right eye was swollen, and the cheek beneath it had bloated to double its regular size.

"Mama?" I asked again, not sure if it was her beneath all that battered skin.

She reached out and gripped my arms and pulled me up to a seated position. Mindy slipped down to the floor. There was nothing I could do to save her; my Mama's hands were too firmly clenched on to me. Mama started to shake and shake and shake me. Her jaw was set and she said to me through clenched teeth, "It's time you learned, Rhetta. You have to learn sooner or later. It's time you learned. This is what life is."

I started to cry. Not because she was shaking me or because of the things she was saying—I didn't know what she was talking about anyway. I cried because she looked so scary, one eye all puffed around the edges, one cheek swollen like an apple. She looked like a wicked witch or an evil stepmother.

The light clicked on in the hallway, and Grammie's bare feet thumped against the hall carpet. She was at my bedside and prying my Mama's hands from me before I had even registered that she was in the room at all. "Nancy," Grammie was saying. "Nancy. Nancy. Nancy."

And Mama kept wobbling her hands back and forth, even after my arms weren't squeezed inside them anymore. She looked up at Grammie and said, "She's gotta learn, Ma. She's old enough to know the truth."

Grammie was shaking Mama now, holding her arms and rocking her quickly back and forth the way Mama had just been doing with me. She just kept saying Mama's name over and over again: "Nancy. Nancy. Nancy."

Mama dropped her arms to her side and Grammie let go of her. They just stayed like that for a second, Mama sitting on my bed and staring up at Grammie, Grammie standing above her and staring down. After a few seconds, Mama's whole body started to quiver. Then she moaned, a long wailing note that trembled up and down in pitch the way her body trembled. She lowered her head into the palms of her hands and just started sobbing. Strong, angry sobs that looked like they welled up from deep inside and couldn't help but burst out of her in a wild torrent. I had never seen Mama cry before. I honestly hadn't been sure whether she knew how.

Thought maybe that was something that little girls lost when they became big.

Grammie kneeled down in front of Mama and wrapped her arms around her. She was still just saying Mama's name, but she said it in a softer tone now, in the cooing voice she always used with me after I'd had a nightmare. After Mama's sobbing slowed down a bit, Grammie stood back up again and gently pulled Mama to her feet to lead her out of my room with one arm thrown over Mama's back, one hand on Mama's elbow.

I lay back down, pulled the blanket up around me, and listened, wondering what Grammie was saying to Mama now that they were alone in Mama's room. I could hear voices muffled through the wall, but the voices were low and gentle. I couldn't make out what was being said.

Eventually, I heard Mama's door swing closed and then Grammie came back into my room and sat down on my bed. She pulled the blanket up to my chin and then patted it at the sides to be sure it was snug. Then she reached down, picked up Mindy, and slid her under the blanket beside me. "You go right back to sleep now, Rhetta. You never mind your Mama."

"Grammie?" I asked. "What happened to Mama's face?"

She smoothed my hair against my head. "Nothing for you to worry about. She got in a little trouble at work is all."

"Someone hurt her?"

"Nothing for you to worry about, Rhetta." She leaned down and kissed me on the forehead.

"But who hurt her, Grammie?"

Grammie sighed. She looked at the wall that my room shared with Mama's. Just stared at it for a second and then looked back down at me. "Never mind, Rhetta. Your Mama'll be just fine. Go right back to sleep and forget this ever happened, okay? And when you wake up in the morning, I'll make you pancakes. You'll think this was all just a bad dream." She kissed me again and then switched off my lamp and left.

I waited for a second as the stillness of the house settled and then whispered, "Mindy."

I pulled her string, and she whispered back, "What?"

"What do you think happened to Mama?"

I pulled Mindy's string. She said, "My name's Mindy, and I love you." It's what she says when she doesn't want to say anything. She has to speak if someone pulls her string.

"Come on, Mindy. I'm serious."

I pulled her string again, and she said, "Rhetta, it's none of our business."

"But Mama wanted me to know," I said, looking at the wall adjoining my room and Mama's. "What if she needs help?"

When I pulled her string again, Mindy said, "I think we should go back to sleep, like your Grammie said."

I sighed, turned over onto my side, and closed my eyes.

7

When I wake up this morning I just know that I've overslept. I can feel it in my stomach, sinking and cold. I peel my eyes open and want to close them right back up again because the room is spinning and the air seems to be pulsing. I don't want to go to work, but there is nobody to write me a note or call Burt for me. I have to force myself to climb out of bed and pull on a pinafore, braid my hair as best I can and head off.

I did oversleep, I was right, and I don't have time for tea and scones, which offends Mindy when I tell her. I *am* hungry, though, so I stop by this little hut that sells coffee on the way to work. I don't like coffee—tried it once when Grammie was having some and it was the most disgusting, mucky thing I've ever had—but the hut also sells donuts and things. I order a donut, a breakfast burrito, and a sausage rolled pancake on a stick. The first two I leave in the little white paper bag the lady gives me, but the pancake I nibble as I walk the rest of the way to work. It's so good I want to just gobble it all down, but I hold myself back because once it's gone, it's gone, and I don't have time to go back and get another.

By the time I get to the office, I'm exactly five minutes late. Michael was nice about me getting him in trouble with Burt, but there's got to be a limit to what one person will put up with. At school, back before Grammie pulled me out, they used to close the doors and lock them when the bell would ring. If you weren't in your seat, you had to knock so the teacher could stop what he was doing and let you in. Sometimes the teacher would make an example of the kids who were late. At work, I'm sure being late is even less acceptable. I know Michael won't close the cubicle door—because the cubicle doesn't have a door, for one thing—but that doesn't mean he won't make an example of me in front of the entire office. Or Burt might do it.

When I step into the cubicle, I see that Michael isn't even here. His desk is empty and his coat isn't hanging over the back of his chair like it usually is. By some miracle, Michael happens to be late on the same day that I am. I pull Mindy out of my purse and smile at her. She winks at me. Everything always works out in the end, she's thinking. I have to stifle a giggle because I'm so delighted to find out that it's true.

I know I should dive right into my claims, be busily at work already whenever Michael shows up, but I still have a donut and a breakfast burrito in that baggie, and suddenly nothing seems more important—not work or Michael's opinion of me or even the prospect of getting yelled at by Burt—as eating until I can't eat anymore. Mindy watches me closely as I pull the little bag open and take out its contents—the donut, then the burrito—and lay them in front of me on my desk.

I glance up at Mindy and catch her eye. A mistake, because now that I've made eye contact with her I can't pretend that I don't see how much she disapproves. If I pulled her string right now, she would say she's upset because this is fast food, and Grammie always said fast food is bad for you. But I know the truth is that she's offended that I'm eating something else, something that she didn't conjure up for me.

But my stomach is churning, growling noisily. The sausage pancake on the way here seems only to have made me hungrier, and the sweet smell of the donut and the greasy smell of the burrito—it's maddening. I either have to eat this food right now or completely destroy it somehow. In a few minutes I won't be able to make the choice anymore. I'll just gulp it all down without even thinking about Mindy's feelings.

And then, thankfully, a diversion shows up. Michael. He whistles as he walks into our cubicle and swings a blue plastic bag back and forth in his right hand. He sets the bag on his desk—gently, like it's a fragile treasure—and then he turns to me and nods as he takes off his jacket. "Morning, Rhetta."

"Morning, Michael," I say. "You're late."

He laughs. "I'm sorry. I got halfway here and then," he pauses, looks down at the bag and smiles, "and then remembered something I wanted to bring in. Had to go back for it."

I look at the bag, then down at the food in front of me. "I brought you some breakfast," I say. "What would you rather have: the burrito or the donut?" I pick them up and hold them out to him.

The red crawls all over his face and he reaches out to take the donut. "Thanks. That was really thoughtful."

I pull down the foil on the burrito, trying to avoid glancing at Mindy, and take a bite. "What's in the bag?" I ask Michael after I swallow.

"Oh, nothing," he says. "Just something I bought for my desk." His eyes glint, his smile deepens, and I know something special is about to happen. He looks like a magician about to do the big reveal.

He sits down, picks up the bag, and then spins his chair around to face me.

"What is it?" I ask. "Come on. Show me."

He reaches his hand into the bag, grabs hold of whatever it is that's inside and then pauses, grinning, before he slowly pulls it out. A little tuft of black hair. A plastic face. A doll. A little boy doll.

I squeal and clap my hands, involuntarily bounce up and down in my chair. "Where'd you get him?"

"You like him?" Michael asks, holding the doll on his lap and turning him over, inspecting him from all sides.

"Are you kidding? I love him!"

"I found him at a garage sale," he says. "Doesn't he look just like your doll?" He holds the little boy up to Mindy. He's right; the new doll looks a lot like Mindy. His rosy cheeks, his stiff black hair, his purple eyes. They could be twins, or at least, he could be Mindy's much younger brother. Even though Michael says he found him used, the doll still looks brand new, unplayed with.

"What's his name?" I ask.

"Ralph," Michael says.

I wrinkle my nose and stick out my tongue.

Michael laughs. "I know. It's the name he came with."

81

"Well, Ralph," I say. "It's very nice to meet you." I shake his tiny plastic hand.

Michael pulls the string on Ralph's back. In a mechanical, emotionless voice, Ralph says, "My name's Ralph. Let's be friends."

I laugh. "He is just like Mindy."

I pick up Mindy and pull her string. "My name's Mindy, and I love you."

Michael sits Ralph down on his desk, in front of the row of angry men and directly across from Mindy. "They seem to be hitting it off well."

I can't say that I agree. Mindy just sits there staring at Ralph, and Ralph just stares back, but in a vacant way. I nod anyway, though, and say, "Yep. I think they'll be good friends."

Later, when Michael says he has to go talk to Burt, I check to make sure no one's looking and then kneel down in front of Ralph and ask him, "Ralph? Are you real?"

I pull the little string on his back. "Let's have some fun."

I look at Mindy, who is watching us from my desk. She just stares solemnly at Ralph.

I pull Ralph's string again. "You're my best friend."

I move back to my seat and meet Mindy's purple gaze.

"Maybe Michael will make him real," I whisper, but I don't pull her string because I know what she would say already, and I don't want to hear her say it.

8

Ralph makes Mindy feel uncomfortable—It's like having a dead thing, she says, sitting across the way—but I like him. Like the way Michael tried to interact with him all day long, how he'd shake his hand, or how he offered Ralph a fry during lunch. Michael is so gentle with Ralph. Michael's hands, which are not dry and cracked like Mama always told me men's hands are, look so soft against the smooth plastic of Ralph's skin. I can't help but wonder what Michael's hands must feel like, what his skin would feel like against my skin.

I'm thinking about it as I sip my tea and only half listening as Mindy tells me all the reasons why she doesn't think this Ralph thing is a good idea, but then Mindy says something that catches my attention. She says, "Ralph is just like your Mama's doll, Rhetta" and I feel the bottom drop out of my stomach.

Mama came home from work early one day, kicked off her shoes, and slumped over on the sofa. Just sat there, her arms folded and her head leaning back against the cushion, staring at me and Mindy and Grammie, all three of us sitting on the floor playing stuffed animals.

Mindy sat on my lap as I moved a fat stuffed tabby cat up and down on the floor in front of me. Grammie had given it to me after I had begged and pleaded for a real pet cat. "Toy cats are more fun," Grammie had told me. "You don't have to feed them or take out their litter."

Grammie held a giant elephant out in front of her in one hand. She bounced the elephant up and down and this way and that, her other hand stretched behind her to rub her lower back.

Mama looked down at us from her perch on the sofa and stared, expressionless.

"But I'm afraid of cats," Grammie made the elephant say in her best impression of a deep voice.

I laughed. I always laughed when Grammie did that voice. It didn't suit her, and her face would get all scrunched up when she would do it. "But I'm a nice cat," I made my tabby say. "I like to dance and play and sing. La la la la la."

Grammie laughed and dropped the elephant, covering her mouth with her hand and shaking her head. "Oh mercy."

Mama cleared her throat. It was meant as a warning. Both Grammie and I looked up at Mama, looking down at us.

"Nancy, would you like to play?" Grammie said in a suddenly crisp voice.

Mama didn't say anything, just looked from Grammie to me and then, finally, to Mindy, her eyes narrowed into tiny slits. And then she stood up, swooped down and grabbed Mindy from my lap.

"Hey!"

But Mama dangled Mindy above me by one arm and shook her at me. "You're too old for this shit."

"Nancy," Grammie said.

Mama turned to Grammie. "She's too old, Ma."

"She's eight, Nancy."

"Eight's too old. You wanna know why she doesn't have any friends?" She shook Mindy hard and I cringed, afraid that Mindy's arm would snap in two from the weight of her hanging body. Mama turned to me. "I'm sorry, Rhetta. It's for your own good." And Mama carried Mindy down the hall and into her bedroom, and closed the door.

I turned to Grammie, my eyes welling with tears. "Grammie," I said, but it came out choked, so I tried again. "Gr-Grammie." But I couldn't get any further than that.

Grammie slid the elephant and cat away with her arms and scooped me onto her lap, heaving a little as she did it. "Shh, now, shh, baby. It's okay. Your Grammie'll get her back,

I promise." With me clutching at her neck, she stood up and carried me into my bedroom, laid me down and tucked me in and kissed me gently on the cheek. Then she walked into Mama's room and closed the door.

I couldn't hear much through the wall. Mostly I could just hear the sound of my heartbeat throbbing in my ears and my own gasps for air between sobs. By the time Grammie carried Mindy back in, I had cried myself to sleep already, my arms wrapped around my pillow where Mindy should have been. I woke up as Grammie slid Mindy under the covers beside me.

"Mindy," I said and kissed her over and over and over again. "Grammie, you got her."

Grammie nodded and brushed her fingertips across my forehead. "Don't listen to your Mama, Rhetta. Eight isn't too old."

"I know," I said. "Mama's so mean."

Grammie didn't say anything.

"She's just jealous because Mindy doesn't like her."

Grammie kissed me and then Mindy on our foreheads. "She won't do it again, I promise."

"She will too," I said, looking at Mindy again. "She hates Mindy because I love her."

"Ah, Rhetta, your Mama doesn't mean any harm."

"Yeah huh, Grammie. Mama's like the witch in Snow White. She hates Mindy. She wants to tear out her heart and eat it."

Grammie's face contorted. "Rhetta, wherever did you hear such a thing?"

"I read it."

"Where?"

I shrugged, then yawned.

85

She shook her head. "Get some rest, sweetheart. Don't you worry about your Mama. She just had a hard night is all. She doesn't mean anything by it."

After Grammie left, I pulled Mindy's string because I knew she was probably just dying to tell me what had happened, but all she could do at first was let out a stifled moan. Then she said, "Oh, Rhetta. It's terrible."

"What is?"

She wrapped her arms around my neck and cried.

"What is it, Mindy?"

She regained control of herself and said, "She threw me in the closet. On the shoes."

I nodded. I understood. With the blond haired doll, the one with the empty eyes.

"That doll," she said and moaned again. "She's dead, Rhetta."

"What do you mean?"

Mindy nodded. "It isn't that she was never alive. It's that she's dead."

My body felt cold all over. "How do you know?" I asked.

But when I pulled her string again she just said, "She was going to do it to me, I know it. That's why she took me. She was going to kill me, too."

I squeezed Mindy tight and slinked all the way under the covers with her. Mama was evil. She was some kind of witch. I had always known it on some level, but now I knew it for sure. She wanted to hurt me and Mindy. All we had to protect us was Grammie. I could only hope that Grammie would never give in.

9

I'm really getting the hang of this denial thing. It's a riddle, a sort of equation like the ones Grammie used to have me practice after she pulled me out of school. She bought all these secondhand workbooks and reading primers, ones that had other children's notes scrawled in the margins, and she made me do my lessons for an hour every day. But I usually did them for longer because I liked them, and I liked the Maths best of all. That was what the workbook called it: Maths.

Denials, it turns out, are like the Maths equations that would give you a little story and have you figure out some embedded equation. Jenni, David, and Tom are taking the train to the city, but Jenni doesn't get on the train until an hour after David, and so on. It's like that only they're real people, and the numbers in the equation represent real money—the company's money—which we need to hang on to as best we can. Bryr Lubbock has a pinched sciatic nerve. It will cost the company $1,000 if we pay for the chiropractor her doctor, Hans Beck, has referred her to. But chiropractors don't practice scientific medicine, and this referral is to alleviate the pain rather than fix the problem. If we approve this referral, even with a, say, three visit limit, Doctor Hans may refer more patients to this chiropractor, this chiropractor may attempt to bill us for future visits, and if nothing else, the company will be out $1,000. Denied.

It's fun once you really get into the spirit of it, and it's rewarding to see that stack of denials at the end of the workday. It's a completely different feeling than when I finish a coloring book or put together a complete building out of blocks. Those feel good for a second, but then you realize that the book is finished and has to be tucked into Grammie's box of "Rhetta's Finished Coloring Books," or the building, as imposing as it is, has to be taken down again so you can build something else with the blocks.

Anyway, I've come to really like this job, and it isn't just because I like Michael. But I do like Michael; I don't care what Mindy says. I've come to look forward to the day ahead when I get up in the morning. Even the mornings where I feel sort of sick, which is getting to be most of them, like today. I wake up dizzy and nauseated. My legs feel frail, like they can barely carry my weight, and so I just want to get to the office as quickly as possible. When I get to the building, there are all these people standing around outside. My eyes go fuzzy for a second, not sure if I'm at the right place.

They're marching around in an extended oval and holding signs above them in the air. Poster boards with hand-written messages on them. Some of them are yelling. At first I can't make it out—they're all yelling something different, and their voices merge together into the sound of nonsense—but when I step a little closer and watch them circle past me I see that they are yelling variations of the things written on their signs.

"People should not be DENIED the right to live!"

"The terminally ill are people, too!"

And the most disturbing one. "May my husband's death haunt you forever!"

I veer around the people and make my way over to the stairs, but they notice me, of course, and one of them, a man, calls out: "Hey, lady! You do business with murderers?"

I can feel Mindy shifting around in my purse. I know that she wants me to keep going. Ignore them. It's what Grammie would tell me to do. Look the other way, Rhetta. Just look the other way and keep walking.

I turn around and say, "I'm sorry. I don't have time for this." Polite but firm. Very grown-up of me.

The man rests the sign on his shoulder and cocks his head. "Oh really? And why's that?"

I look around the group of people. They've stopped marching and are all turned to face me. Staring, some of them glaring, and all of them waiting for me to respond. I know that they must already know why I'm outside this building at eight in the morning. They want me to say, "I work here," so they can pelt me with rocks—I read about that in one of Mama's books—or maybe they'll beat me with their signs. My eyes are going fuzzy again; my legs are so tired. The people are starting to pulse in and out, and my heart is thump-thumping so loud in my chest it's drowning everything out. The man says something, I hear it like it's muffled through a wall, and then he sneers, lifts the sign up high into the air in front of me.

A woman steps forward from the crowd. She's coming at me, running, and I think she's yelling something too, but I can't hear her at all. After that, there's nothing. Darkness. But the darkness is still spinning somehow. Going in and out in shades of grey. And there's a smacking sound—thwap thwap thwap thwap—like the darkness is hitting something just outside my field of vision.

Everything begins to converge together again, and I suddenly know, in a deep down kind of way, that my eyes have been open this whole time but weren't seeing. And the back of my head is throbbing.

The woman, the one who was running at me a moment ago, is kneeling above me and shrieking. "Are you okay? Answer me! Answer me, are you okay?"

I open my mouth to speak, but nothing comes out. I nod, start to sit up, but hands all around me push me back down.

89

"Are you epileptic?" a man's voice asks.

I don't say anything at first. Then, from the way everyone's staring down at me, I realize the question is directed at me. "Um," I say, and my tongue feels thick in my mouth. "No."

"Do you work here?" the woman asks, and there is no animosity in her voice. This is not a trick question.

I nod.

"We're going to see if we can get some help," the woman says.

I look all around me. All the signs are lying abandoned on the ground, and the people stand over me, their looks of anger completely gone. Some of them look almost scared.

"What happened?" I ask.

"You looked like you were having a seizure," the woman says. "You were banging your head on the cement."

"And your eyes," a man says. "They were just sort of . . . staring."

"Is Mindy okay?" But I remember immediately that they won't know who that is.

"It's okay, honey," the woman says. She swipes her hand across my forehead. It feels like something Grammie would have done. "We'll get you to the hospital."

"No, I'm okay," I say and prop myself up on my elbows. "Really. I just tripped."

The woman exchanges a dark look with the man next to her, but neither one of them says anything.

Then I hear footsteps beating against the pavement. It's Michael and Burt, rushing outside with a man from the crowd who must have gone inside to get them.

Michael reaches out and helps me to my feet. "What the fuck did you guys do?" he yells.

"Sir, she should lie down," someone says.

Michael pulls me close to him, puts his arm around me, and my head drops down to his shoulder. I can smell his neck, a tangy, minty smell. "You okay, Rhetta?"

"I just tripped," I say again. It doesn't seem like anybody hears me.

Burt is standing with his arms folded, glaring at the people. "You folks going to leave peaceably, or am I going to have to call the police?"

"We didn't touch her," a man's voice says.

But the woman who had been leaning over me shakes her head. "We'll go. We didn't touch her, but we don't want any trouble."

Burt nods. "A wise decision," he says. "Probably the wisest thing any one of you ever said."

I hear the clatter of footsteps and people mumbling, but Michael is already slowly leading me inside. He walks with me pulled close to his side, one arm firmly around my shoulder, and leads me to our cubicle. He sits me down in a chair. I feel like a doll. This must be how it feels to be Mindy.

He squats down in front of me, one hand resting on my desk, and asks, "Are you going to be okay? Do you need to go to the hospital?"

I smile. I can't help it. It feels so good to hear the concern in his voice. "I'm fine."

"What happened?" he asks.

"I don't know. I just felt sort of dizzy."

"It's the adrenaline," Burt's voice booms over us.

Michael stands up and sits down in his chair.

"Probably got a mean rush from those punks," Burt says. He hands me my purse, which I must have dropped outside, and

Mindy's weight inside it feels heavy as the straps drop into my hands. "What did they say to you, Rhetta?"

"Uh, nothing," I say. I know it's a lie, but I suddenly can't remember what they did say. "I'm just not feeling well today. It was just a coincidence."

Burt hmmphs and then says, "You need to take a day off?" But I can hear in his voice that it's not a genuine offer. That there is a right answer to this question, and the right answer is no.

"I think I'll be okay." I pat the waiting claims on my desk. "Got work to do."

His lips turn up into a little half smile, but all he says is, "Well enough," and walks away.

After he leaves, I turn around and pull Mindy out of my purse, but before I can inspect her for damage, Michael rolls his chair over to me. "They said you were having a seizure," he says.

Without meaning to, I touch the back of my head, which still pulses in unspeakable pain. "No."

Michael narrows his eyes. "Are you sure you don't want to go to the hospital?"

I shake my head.

He sighs and leans back in his chair, his eyes still focused on me. "Anything like this ever happen before?"

"No," I say, too quickly. "I mean. I think I'm coming down with something. I've just been feeling a little off lately."

"Rhetta, if you're sick you should go home."

The thought of turning around and walking all the way home . . . I don't think I can do it right now. "I'm feeling much better."

He seems unconvinced, but he shrugs anyway and rolls his chair back over to his desk.

I turn Mindy over in my hands, feeling for bruises, but she seems okay. I give her a long, tight hug. Michael turns around and catches me in the act, so I quickly set Mindy down, faking a laugh. "I was worried she might have broken or something. I'm just relieved."

He nods. "Her voicebox okay?"

I pull her string. "Come on, let's play," her mechanical voice says.

Michael laughs. "Good news."

"I would be devastated if anything happened to her," I say. "She was a present from my Grammie, you know. When I was little." I pause and then add, "She's dead now."

"I'm so sorry," he says.

"She was really old," I say. "I think she was in her fifties. At least."

He furrows his brow. "Fifty isn't all that old."

"Well maybe sixties then. I don't know."

He doesn't say anything for a second, and when he does, his voice is kind of husky. "Rhetta, you know, if she died of something . . . specific . . ." But then he just sighs and says, "Never mind."

For a second all I can think about is creeping down the hallway, hearing the alarm clock screeching over and over, the creak of Grammie's door as I swung it open, and then, her body lying motionless in the bed, her face all soft, the muscles just drooping under the skin, and her thin silver hair surrounding her head like a halo.

"She wasn't sick or anything," I say, but I'm really just thinking aloud now. "Not that I know of. But I guess I could picture her not telling me if she was."

He nods.

"Anyway, I don't think there's anything running in the family. I think my Mama died really young, but I'm pretty sure she killed herself." I avoid catching Mindy's gaze.

"I'm so sorry," Michael says. "How old were you?"

"Eight," I say. "My Grammie raised me."

"Your Grammie didn't tell you how your mom died?"

"My Grammie didn't even tell me that she died," I say. "I figured it out on my own."

"Wow, that's . . . that's really weird." He looks down at the stack of claims on his desk.

I look at Ralph and then at Michael. "Hey, Michael. Do you think you and Ralph might be interested in coming over for tea sometime? Saturday night, maybe?"

The red spider webs appear on Michael's cheeks and neck. He keeps his face turned down as he says, "We would love to."

10

I pour the tea into Mindy's little cup and then my own. Mindy just sits staring at me as I reach forward and grab a shortbread cookie, dip it into my tea and take a small bite. It tastes like nothing. Just disappears in my mouth.

It isn't that I'm trying to ignore Mindy exactly; it's just that I know what she wants to tell me, about how it was a mistake, inviting Michael and Ralph over, about how it's dangerous and stupid. But being with Michael doesn't feel dangerous. It feels exciting, feels right.

Mindy doesn't like the questions he was asking today. She says I shouldn't think about Grammie's death and those daunting first few weeks alone, just me and Mindy. She doesn't think it's healthy to dwell in the shadows of the past. But now that Michael's brought it up, it feels impossible that this stuff doesn't matter, Mama and Grammie and everything that's come since.

Like the fact that after I found Grammie's body, I had no idea what you do when someone dies, so I just stood there, staring and crying and holding myself the way I wanted Grammie to hold me. Part of me even wanted to climb in the bed with her, to wrap my arms around her and nestle my head underneath her chin. But part of me was scared of her face, how it looked all melted and empty, and her eyes, which were open but dull and blank.

I didn't know whether I was supposed to close her eyes, put something over them to weigh them down like I had read about in a book one time, and so I didn't even try. Instead I just left the room and closed the door, walked back down the hallway and into the kitchen, where I had been sitting at the table with Mindy just a minute before, waiting for Grammie to come in, make herself some coffee, and get out the cereal and milk for me like usual.

Mindy was sitting on the table with her back leaning against a tucked in chair and her stiff plastic arms outstretched in front of her. Her purple glass eyes stared at me as I walked back into the kitchen. I rushed to the table and picked her up, pressed my wet cheek against her dry plastic one and told her about Grammie. That Grammie was dead.

After I had cried into Mindy's stiff hair for what felt like forever, I remembered a story I had read once where somebody died and they called the police. I tried to get control of myself first, and then I did the same. "Um, hi," I said through stifled sobs when the operator answered. My voice quavered and its pitch was high, higher than usual, and I had to consciously slow my words down so that the operator could understand me.

"My name's Rhetta. I don't know what to do. It's my Grammie. I think she's dead."

"I'm so sorry, sweetheart," the operator said in a soft tone. "Tell me, are there any adults around?"

I glanced around the room for some reason, even though I knew there was nobody else in the house but me and Mindy and my Grammie's dead body. "No," I said. "It's just me and my doll."

"It was very brave of you to call," the operator said. "You must be a very brave girl. How old are you, hon?"

"I'm thirty," I said.

There was a pause before the operator said, "Come again?"

"Thirty," I said again. "Well, thirty and a half."

Another pause. All trace of sympathy had drained from her voice by the time she said, "Give me your address. I'll send someone right over."

I washed my face and braided my hair. Then I put on my nicest pink pinafore and sat down on the couch in the living room with Mindy on my lap. Just sat there and waited for the police to come and tell me what to do. After the police came and went, and after the people came and took Grammie's body away, the house was really quiet. Even so, I kept thinking I heard something coming from Grammie's room. Someone coughing. Her closet door sliding open. But I was afraid to go in and check. I was afraid to go down the hallway at all, even though the bathroom was down there next to Grammie's door. When I had to pee, I held it for as long as I could, and when I couldn't hold it any longer, I went out to the backyard and crouched down by a tree. Other than that, though, Mindy and I just sat in the living room and held each other and cried.

After a while, I fell asleep. When I woke up, I realized that I was hungry—famished, in fact—so I went into the kitchen and ate all the candy and the ice cream and the last batch of cookies that Grammie made before she died. And then I ate everything else but the stuff like the flour and the herbs and things. Just stood there in the kitchen and ate and ate and ate. Later, I felt sick and threw up in the backyard.

After that I didn't want to go back to just sitting on the couch, so I decided to rearrange the furniture. That doesn't sound like fun, and it wasn't, but I didn't like to look at all Grammie's stuff. It wasn't even just that it made me think of Grammie and miss her, although it did. But it felt haunted, too. Like everything that had ever belonged to Grammie had captured deep inside it a piece of Grammie's soul. So I moved it all into her bedroom and the other back room, the one that used to be Mama's. But the house felt big and empty with Grammie gone and all her furniture and stuff hidden away, so I moved everything from my bedroom out to the living room. My tea set, my red wooden table, my bed. I moved it all into the living room to help fill in the space.

That night I had to push my bed into the middle of the living room because I kept thinking I saw things crawling on the walls, and there seemed to be noises coming from the hallway. Creaking sounds, and creeping ones, and that pop that happens when somebody steps on just the right part of the floor.

I had to go to the bathroom the first night, had to go real bad but I was scared of walking down the hallway. I was scared, too, of what might happen when I got there. That the door to Grammie's bedroom might swing open and she would stumble out, her eyes opening and closing and opening again.

"Mindy," I whispered and shook her awake.

She looked up at me.

"I have to pee," I whispered and glanced nervously at the hallway. "What should I do?"

I pulled her string, and she whispered, "I'll go with you."

I pulled the covers down, swung my feet over the edge of the bed and hesitated, worried that there might be something hiding under the bed just waiting for an ankle to claw or to bite. But the tingly feeling was getting worse so I put my feet down and scooped Mindy into my arms.

I turned on the light in the hallway and stared down at Grammie's closed door on the other end. I didn't hear anything or see anything either, but I couldn't move, couldn't make one foot go in front of the other and just walk.

I looked down at Mindy.

She reached her tiny hand up and rubbed it against my cheek.

I looked back down the hallway. Nothing had changed. I squeezed Mindy a little tighter and took a deep breath, took a cautious step toward the bathroom. I took another step, then another, then another, and then I heard that popping sound that comes from the floor board. Only it wasn't under my foot. It sounded like it was behind me.

I spun around and stared back at the living room, but nothing was there. I looked down at Mindy again. She smiled up at me. I turned around and stared again at my Grammie's door, kept my eyes focused on it and walked slowly the rest of the way to the bathroom.

As soon as I got there I flicked on the light, rushed inside, and closed and locked the door behind me. I set Mindy down on the sink and peed, staring at the locked door the entire time. When I finished, I picked Mindy back up and stood for a second, my hand hovering over the doorknob. "Did you hear something?" I whispered.

Mindy shook her head.

I looked back at the doorknob, unlocked it, wrapped my fingers around it and stopped again. "I think I felt it move," I whispered.

Mindy squirmed in my arms. I looked down. She was pointing at her back, so I pulled her string. "It's going to be okay. I would never let anything happen to you."

I nodded and opened the door, turned off the bathroom light and walked carefully back down the hallway, pressing Mindy's little plastic body against my racing heart. When I reached the end of the hallway I swung back around, took one last triumphant look at my Grammie's closed door, and turned the light back off.

I climbed into bed and pulled the covers up around Mindy and me. She nuzzled her nub of a nose in my neck, and I whispered to her, "I love you, Mindy."

"I love you, too, Rhetta. I love you so much."

I closed my eyes and sank into the mattress and drifted back off again to sleep.

11

I'm feeling a bit lightheaded this evening, but I don't call Michael and reschedule. Instead, I try to distract myself from the vertigo by setting up the tea set. A setting for me, one for Mindy, one for Michael, and one for Ralph. Mindy and Ralph, I've already decided, will sit next to each other. Michael and I will sit side by side, too. "Boy, girl, boy, girl," I tell Mindy as she eyes the little place settings I made out of construction paper and crayons.

She motions for me to pull her string, but I pretend I don't notice, move swiftly around her, and begin arranging the empty serving platters in the center of the table. "Now, Mindy," I say without looking at her, "I want this to be a very special night. I think we should have as many different kinds of cakes and cookies and things as we can, and I think we should have flavored tea. Raspberry, maybe."

I see movement out of my periphery, but I don't turn, don't pull her string. I just finish setting up, and then, when there's nothing else I could possibly busy myself with, I sit down on the bed and fold my hands in my lap to wait.

It will be like it was when Grammie was around, I just know it. Michael will understand my relationship with Mindy, and Mindy will come to understand Michael. She'll come to love him. And she'll love Ralph, too. Ralph will become real—he's the kind, I know he is—and we'll be just like a real family, Mindy and Ralph will be brother and sister, Michael and I will be parents, lovers. It's clear to me now that my whole life has been building to this. To Michael. To real love. The kind I've read about in too many books to count. The kind Mama used to fake with the men at the club.

Maybe Ralph will even become real tonight. Once I tell Michael the truth about Mindy, Ralph might turn his face up, his little neck popping the way Mindy's once did. We'll pull his string together, Michael's hand wrapped around mine wrapped around the string, and Ralph will say, "Hello, Mother," with tears welling in his eyes.

Michael and Ralph will be here soon, but the room is spinning. I need to rest my eyes for a second. Need to be ready when they show up because we've got a big night ahead of us, we all do, and I don't want to be feeling sick like this. Don't want to pass out again.

"Soon Ralph will be real," I say to Mindy and lie down on top of the blanket, drop my head to the pillow. The bed shifts a bit as Mindy climbs onto my stomach. I keep my eyes closed and say, "Won't that be nice?" But I don't pull her string so she can answer.

100

12

It happened when I was six. I invited Mindy to tea, and she gracefully accepted my invitation with a, "Come on, let's play," which I interpreted as an eager "yes." There were only three things she could say back then, so it took some imaginative thinking sometimes to make it all fit together. Make it mean what I thought it should.

So I pulled the blue and pink striped cardboard box that housed my tea set from underneath my bed. I laid it on my comforter, pulled open the lid, and carefully took out item after item. The tiny blue saucers with their matching blue plastic cups. The small plastic kettle with its delicately curving spout. The little blue plates that I always pretended were brimming with cakes, cookies, muffins, and sweet breads.

As I pulled out the sugar bowl, I heard a rustling noise over at the table, where I had set Mindy down in one of the little chairs to wait. I whirled around, sure that the rustling sound had come from that direction. Mindy sat at the table and stared straight ahead. Her body still new and stiff, she didn't bend all the way when she sat, so she was leaning at an odd angle against the red chair's hearted back. Her hands were up on the table. I didn't think that I had set her hands like that, but I wasn't sure.

I stood still and watched her for a few seconds. She didn't do anything, so I turned back around to continue getting the tea set ready. "Mindy," I called back to her, "why don't you come help me carry this stuff over?"

I turned around and looked at Mindy sitting there, arms still resting on the table, eyes still blank. I sighed and turned back around, moved everything onto the little serving tray and carried it over to the table.

I laid out the tea set slowly, watching Mindy as I set a little blue plate in front of her, then a saucer and a cup. She didn't move. I walked around to my side of the table, arranged my plate and cup, and then sat down opposite Mindy.

"Care for some tea?" I didn't reach forward for the tea kettle. I wanted to see if Mindy would reach for it herself, but she didn't. "And please," I motioned toward the empty serving plate, "try some shortbread. It's my chef's specialty."

Mindy just stared ahead.

I fiddled with my cup for a second and then stood up and walked over to Mindy. I leaned down so that my face was level with hers and said "Mindy?" in my most pleading tone.

Nothing. I sighed and placed the palms of my hands on the table to brace myself as I stood up. Mindy's neck popped, like joints that had been still far too long. I stopped, my heart pounding. And then her little smiling plastic face turned to me, her purple eyes vibrant, almost glowing. I couldn't see my own reflection in them anymore.

I jumped to my feet and screamed.

A loud thud came from my Mama's room next door. Mindy's head snapped back to its regular position. I ran back to my seat across from Mindy and sat down just in time for Mama to slam my door open and hurry inside.

"What is it? What's wrong?" Her blond hair was pulled tightly into curlers and her face was covered in white and blue clay, which had hardened and begun to crack. She looked like Medusa. The mask covered her entire face, held it stiffly in place, except for two holes around her eyes and one surrounding her lips. When she spoke, the mask crumbled a bit and piled into dust at her feet. "What?" she asked again, stepping forward.

I pressed my body harder against my chair. "I . . . I was calling for Grammie," I said.

Mama folded her arms. "Well you got me."

I looked at Mindy. She sat motionless, staring straight ahead. But her eyes weren't empty. They were looking at me like they were actually seeing me. "Nothing, I just wanted to show Grammie something."

Mama was by my side in a second. She grabbed my chin and squeezed it, pulled it up so I had to look at her. "You do not scream like that just to get somebody's attention."

"I'm sorry," I said.

"You hear me?"

"I'm sorry, Mama."

She let go of my chin and brought the palm of her hand to her forehead. She pulled it back down again, looked at the gritty blue. "You scared me," she said, still looking at her hand. Then she wiped it off on her plaid pajama bottoms, leaving a long blue streak.

"I'm sorry," I said again, trying not to look at the thin patch of skin peeking out on her forehead. It looked like it had its own face, its own two staring little eyes.

"Now what did you want to show Grammie?" she asked, her voice gentler.

I glanced back over at Mindy. She was still watching me. "Um, my chef made shortbread," I said. "Grammie likes shortbread."

Mama shook her head. "Are you kidding me?" She pointed her finger at me. "You do not scream like that just to show somebody imaginary shortbread. You got that?"

"Yes, Mama."

"When a little girl screams like that, grown-ups assume the worst. You've got to learn the difference between reality and make-believe."

I nodded.

After Mama left, I looked across the table at Mindy, who was still looking at me. "Mindy?"

Mindy cocked her head to the side and nodded slowly.

"Mindy," I whispered, "are you a good doll or a evil one?"

She lifted her arm and bent it around to point at the string on her back. The plastic popped as it writhed against itself.

I stood up, walked around the table, and leaned down to pull her string.

Part of me expected her to just say one of the prerecorded statements. But instead of, "My name's Mindy and I love you," or, "Come on, let's play," or, "We're going to be friends forever," Mindy said, "I'm a good doll, Rhetta." Her voice was high and girlish like mine, but it had an undertone of static. It didn't sound like the voice of a real girl, but it didn't sound emotionless either.

I wrapped my arms around her and hugged her as tight as I could. "Grammie said you could become real, but I wasn't completely sure."

She nuzzled her nose into my hair.

After a second, I pulled back and said, "Come on, let's have some tea." I stood up and pushed my chair over next to Mindy's and moved my plate and cup over, too. I picked up the teakettle and felt the heft of something more than hollow plastic. I tilted it to pour the tea into our cups, and I would have known without even looking that the tea wasn't imaginary. I could smell the lemon twirling in the rising steam. "How many sugars?" I asked Mindy.

I pulled Mindy's string, and she said, "Two, please."

I reached for the little sugar bowl I had laid out in the center of the table and found inside sparkling cubes of sugar. Next to the sugar bowl, the plastic plate was piled high with shortbread, cupcakes, and sugar dusted cookies.

"Two?" I asked, dipping the sugar tongs into the bowl and grasping two cubes of sugar.

I pulled Mindy's string with my other hand. "Yes, please. And I'd love to try your chef's special shortbread." Mindy turned her eyes up to me. The purple sparkled with the most amazing play of light and life and happiness and love.

I dropped two sugars into Mindy's cup.

Mindy reached out her plastic hands, which didn't even have separate fingers, just ridges where the fingers would be if she wasn't a doll. She took the cup, which looked more like a bowl in her tiny hands, and lifted it to her mouth to take a slow, careful sip. She lowered the cup to below her chin and smiled, a sheen of translucent brown around her lips.

I tore off a bit of shortbread for Mindy and a bit for myself and said, "Mindy, why didn't you move when my Mama was here?"

I pulled her string. "I don't know, Rhetta. She scares me."

I nodded. "Me too. Sometimes I think she's a witch or something. I think she's out to get me."

The smell of burning plastic filled the air, and I looked back down at my teacup. It seemed to be melting a little from the heat of the tea. The plastic was warping even as I watched, tiny little plastic bubbles forming along the outside of the cup. "Mindy," I said and pointed to her cup.

She looked down and we both watched as the blue plastic softened and stretched, twisted itself out of shape. The edges of both cups curled in on themselves and grew longer, extended and distorted into the sort of teacups you'd expect to see in a nightmare.

"The plastic isn't made for real tea," I told Mindy.

I pulled her string so she could say, "It isn't real tea. It's make-believe tea." She wiped her mouth with the back of her arm and then looked down at it, as if verifying for herself that her statement had been true.

"Whatever it is," I said, "it's too warm."

"That just means we have to drink it fast. I'll race you."

And that was the beginning of the beginning.

13

I must have fallen asleep because when I hear the knock on the door—three quick thumps followed by a deliberate cough—I awaken to a mounting sense of panic. I pop straight up, my head throbbing. The room is spinning, and I don't know at first who would be at the door. Mindy sits up and looks at me.

"Who is it?" I whisper to her.

She doesn't shrug or anything. Doesn't even motion for me to pull her string. I clutch her in my arms and hug her close as I make my way to the door. Just as I reach it there is another succession of knocks, thump-thump-thump, a little more forceful this time. More resolute.

"Who is it?" I call, looking down at Mindy.

There is another cough. Definitely a masculine cough. And then, "It's Michael. Um. Is this Rhetta's house?"

Warmth floods my face, and I swing the door open. "Oh, Michael, I'm so sorry. I fell asleep."

He stands with one hand plunged awkwardly into his jacket pocket, the other holding a brightly colored bouquet of flowers. He glances down at the flowers, then at Mindy in my arms, and the red crawls up his face the fastest I've ever seen.

"Are those for us?" I shift Mindy onto my hip and reach out for the bouquet.

He gives me the flowers and then dips his now empty hand into his other pocket.

I step aside and usher him in. "I'm so sorry about that, Michael. I guess I'm kind of disoriented when I wake up."

He nods, both hands still trapped inside his pockets, and looks around.

I place Mindy in one of the little chairs at the red table and then look around for somewhere to put the flowers. "These are so pretty. I always wondered what it would feel like to get flowers."

Michael chuckles. When he looks at me, though, he immediately stops. The red, which was still lingering from before, deepens around his face and neck.

"So where's Ralph?" I ask.

His face goes blank for a second. Then he smiles and laughs. "Oh. Right. I guess I forgot him."

"You did?" I make an effort not to sound surprised, but I can't mask my disappointment.

He doesn't say anything.

"Doesn't matter," I say. "He'll be mad at you, though."

Michael fakes a laugh, really forces it out, and says, "Right."

"Would you like the grand tour?" I ask.

"Sure," he says, looking around again. "This is so wild. I guess I should have known."

I don't know what he means, so I just ignore the comment. "This is the living room. It's where I, you know, live." I pat my bed. "I guess that's why they call it the living room. And here's the dining room." I point at the table. "And the kitchen's in there, but we don't really use it much. And then down the hall is the bathroom, if you have to go."

107

He blushes, then laughs and shakes his head.

"The bedrooms are down there, too," I tell Michael, "Grammie's and Mama's and my old bedroom."

He looks down the dark hallway. "What do you use the rooms for now?"

"Now?" I glance at Mindy. "Um, nothing. Storage, I guess."

Michael's hands are still inside his jacket pockets, and I can see them clenching and unclenching underneath the fabric.

"Can I take your jacket, Michael?" I reach out for it.

He looks down at his jacket, as though he hadn't even been aware until now that he was wearing it. "Sure," he says, head tilted down. He pulls his hands out of his pockets slowly and unfurls them, then pulls his jacket off and hands it to me.

But now that I have it, I don't actually know what I'm supposed to do with it. In books they always have a cloakroom, or else they go into a bedroom and lay all the coats on the bed. I tenderly drape his jacket on my bed and then step to the table and pull out one of the little red chairs. "Have a seat."

He hesitates before folding his body into the seat. I never noticed until just now how tall Michael is. His legs, which won't even fit underneath the table, stretch up and up and then bend at his knee close to his chin. He twists his body around so he can fold his hands on the table in front of him. He looks funny like this, a grown man at a little girl's table, and it's the first time it's occurred to me that I probably look funny when I sit at the table, too.

"Would you like some tea, Michael?" I ask, picking up the light tea kettle.

Michael's brow furrows as he stares at the plastic kettle. "You put real tea in there?"

"No, silly," I say. "It's make-believe tea." I tilt the spout to pour the raspberry tea into his cup but nothing comes out. I shake the kettle. It's empty.

Michael unfolds his hands and runs his fingers through his hair, then smoothes them over the front of his shirt.

I turn to Mindy and yell, "Tea!"

She just sits there, completely still.

"Michael, I'm so sorry," I turn back to him. "I don't know what is . . ." But the look on his face freezes me, and I can't remember what I was about to say.

His hands are folded beneath his chin now, his elbows resting against his thighs, and he looks up at me with his brow knitted together, his eyebrows raised, and his head tilted slightly to the side. I've seen that look before. On Mama sometimes, and on other people, too. On the policemen who came after Grammie died.

Everything in the room goes hazy but Michael. He's staring right into my eyes, yet his face isn't turning red. I see him, and then I don't see him. One second he's sharp and defined, the next he's hazy. Everything is swirling, blending together—Michael and Mindy and the table and the chairs.

And I'm asleep again. I know that I'm dreaming, but I'm also sitting at the table with Mindy and Ralph. But I'm huge, twice as big as I really am. I look like Alice, dwarfing everything around me. The chair snaps under my weight and I tumble to the floor, but I just laugh and keep drinking the tea. Only it isn't tea. It's just melted plastic. Just a pool of noxious and bubbling melted plastic inside my cup. And Ralph just sits there. And Mindy just sits there.

"Rhetta?" Michael's voice. Everything twists and blurs and then comes back into focus, like a kaleidoscope. He's hovering above me.

I sit up. "Woops," I say, rubbing the back of my head. "Again?" I laugh and shake my head but Michael doesn't join in, doesn't seem to think it's funny.

He helps me to my feet and then onto one of the little red chairs, which suddenly feels unstable. I brace myself, grab the edge of the table to keep from falling down.

"I'll get you something to drink." Michael stands up and looks down at me from above. "And to eat. You should probably eat something, too." He walks into the kitchen, and I hear him opening and closing the cupboard doors.

I lean back against my chair and look at Mindy, who refuses to look at me.

Michael reappears in the entryway from the kitchen and leans against the doorjamb. He opens his mouth like he's going to say something, but nothing comes out. Then he walks back over to the table and kneels down so he's eye level with me. He lays his hands next to mine and asks, "Rhetta, when's the last time you ate?"

I don't say anything.

He sighs and asks, "Do you need me to take you to urgent care?"

Just the thought makes me feel nauseated again. Urgent care, and me without insurance. I've seen the bills those guys send. I know what urgent care would do to me. I shake my head. "I've just been feeling kind of dizzy lately. It's nothing."

But I can tell by the way Michael glances back at my kitchen that he doesn't believe me. "Rhetta," he says, but something, some word I can't make out, gets caught in his throat. He clears it but doesn't try again.

I'm feeling a little better now, the world looks crisp again, and Michael's so close to me I can smell his cologne. Or it might be his deodorant. It smells musky and good. Right now there's

110

nothing in the world that I want more than for him to lean that extra little bit over, to pull me to him and kiss me.

But he doesn't do it. Just clears his throat a second time and then presses his hands against the table as he stands up. "I should let you get some rest," he says. He walks back over to the bed and picks up his jacket, slips it on, and then turns to me, tilts his head. "You sure you won't let me take you to the hospital?"

I look at my feet and shake my head.

He sighs. I don't look up as he walks to the door. His car starts, the gravel in the driveway pops, and he's gone.

I'm still staring at the ground when I hear Mindy climb onto the table and over to me. Her tiny arms wrap around my neck, her light body drops onto my lap, but I keep looking down. I can smell the food on the table now, and the raspberry tea, but I don't want it anymore.

Mindy's weight shifts on my lap. The loop end of her string slides onto my thumb, and then Mindy jumps to the floor, pulling her own string. "You don't need him, Rhetta. You never needed anyone but me."

I wrap my arms around myself and don't say anything.

Mindy climbs back onto my lap and reaches under my chin, lifts it up. Her purple eyes glimmer in the low light. She leans just a little bit closer, grasps the sides of my head with her hands and pulls me closer, kisses me. But her lips are hard and stiff, and I pull away.

"Mindy," I say, but I feel like I'm saying it to myself more than anything. "I think we should get ready for bed."

I pick her up and carry her to the bed, holding her out in front of me but not looking at her. I feel right now like I want to be alone, but Mindy wouldn't understand that wish, and even if she did, she couldn't grant it to me.

I pull off my clothes and slip my nightie over my head. "I'm tired," I say over my shoulder, still without looking directly at her.

I hear the blanket fold back and know that Mindy has tucked herself in. She's waiting for me to climb in beside her, wrap my arms around her and drift away to sleep as though nothing happened.

"I'm going to the bathroom," I say, and I walk all the way down the hallway and close and lock the bathroom door before I realize that this is the first time since Grammie's death I've come down here alone. And I don't even have to go. I put my hands on the counter and rest my weight on it as I look at my reflection in the mirror, try to see what Michael saw before he ran away.

My cheeks are hollow, and the skin underneath my eyes is sunken and dark. My face looks like a skull with a thin layer of fabric stretched taut over the bones. It's the first time in my life I've really looked at myself, and I see, at last, that I am ugly. I look like an old hag, an evil witch with wispy hair, thin skin and empty eyes. I look like I died years ago and nobody ever told me, just let me keep walking around a corpse, an empty bag of skin and bones.

"You're such a pretty girl," I say to my reflection and laugh. Because I look, also, like Grammie. Like she did when I found her limp body that day. But my laughter sounds hysterical, even to my own ears, and my reflection looks scary like this, thin lips drawn into an oval, sunken eyes shining. I look down and take long, deep breaths until I gain control of myself again.

"Michael could never love me," I say into the sink. And then, as though the sink asked for an explanation, I add, "Nobody could ever love me but Grammie and Mindy." But the sink seems unconvinced, so I lift my hands away. Before I can steady myself, my body begins to tilt to the side.

The next thing I'm aware of is a loud banging sound. I look around and see that the bathroom has turned upside down. But that isn't right. It's not the bathroom, it's me. I'm on the floor now, looking up at the ceiling, and my head is throbbing the way it did the other day. It's throbbing and wet and warm and sticky.

The edge of the bathtub is streaked with red. I reach up and touch the viscous substance running down my face, but I don't bother to hold my fingers in front of my eyes and verify what it is. I already know that it's blood the same way I knew, all those years ago, that the tea in my plastic cups was real and somehow not real all at once.

I don't bother to try to lift myself up. Don't really see the point. I just lie here and stare up at the ceiling, which is so smooth it looks like a movie screen. I've only been to a few movies. Grammie stopped taking me after we went to see something, I don't remember what, that she said was inappropriate. She said the ratings board had given in to big business interests and couldn't be trusted to protect the children of the world. But I remember the screens, liquidy and blank as we waited for the projector to kick on and the previews to begin. And that's what the ceiling looks like now. In fact, I think that's exactly what it is. Something is sputtering into life across its surface. I squint and lift my head slightly up to get a better view.

It's me. When I was a little girl. And I can tell right away in some unexplainable way that it's me on the day Grammie gave me Mindy. I rest my head against the floor—it's too much strain trying to hold it up—and watch what I suppose is a hallucination flicker across my bathroom ceiling.

In the beginning she was just a doll, just an ordinary doll like any other doll. A doll with hollow limbs made of plastic and lead-free paint and a chest filled not with a heart but a mechanical voice box activated by a string. She came wrapped up in a box with a huge black bow. The bow was beautiful,

113

immense and satiny, but it turned out to be made in a factory somewhere and affixed to the package with tape, not carefully laced around the box and tied firmly by my Grammie's arthritic fingers.

But it didn't matter because, oh, Mindy dazzled me, with her eyes so purple and her long straight hair so black, like the darkness you wake up to after a nightmare. She came up to my knees back then—I was only five—and the little string on her back felt like it extended forever when I pulled it to hear those first words. "My name's Mindy, and I love you."

I loved her back immediately. How easy it is, at five, to love.

And then Grammie told me all about dolls, how some dolls are different than others. Some can become real. Mindy, she told me, was that kind, and if I tried hard enough, if I believed, the magic would work its way into Mindy's heart and she would come to life.

Now, all these years later, I lie on the bathroom floor in a growing puddle of my own blood and watch my younger self vow to do whatever it would take. I wanted to live in a world where dolls could be real, where little girls could stay little girls forever.

I close my eyes. I don't need to see what happened next. I remember well enough.

I kissed Mindy on her brand new lips and pulled her string a second time and then a third. She said, "Come on, let's play." She said, "We're going to be friends forever."

INTERLUDE

THE THINGS WE TAKE
AND THE THINGS WE LEAVE BEHIND

His boxes are neatly packed and there are only three of them, each labeled with a number that corresponds to a detailed list in his wallet—handwritten as he filled each box and then typed after each item had been carefully categorized and alphabetized. My boxes are overstuffed, bowing out at their cardboard walls and overflowing at their tops, and there are far too many of them. Many more than three, which was the number we agreed on two months ago.

He says I am materialistic.

I say he is heartless.

Because he'd have to be to get rid of the pocket watch that his grandfather gave him. Or to donate to charity the afghan that his mother gave to both of us as a wedding present, which she designed and knitted herself. Or to throw away the card that his coworkers were willing to spend a few uncomfortable minutes staring down at, agonizing over what awkward thing to say, like signing a high school yearbook: "Good luck." "Keep in touch." "It's been great knowing you."

I wonder what says more about you: the things you keep or the things you throw away.

Me, I've gone through my stuff. I told him I've gone through all of it countless times. I can't get rid of any more. This is my history. This is who I am.

My favorite childhood stuffed animal: a gorilla, worn threadbare now and with scratches covering her eyes. Every birthday card my grandparents ever sent me, including the two years in a row where they thought I turned ten, neither of which I did. The collar that my cocker spaniel used to wear before he got cancer and had to be put down, and especially the little heart shaped tag hanging from the collar with his name and mine engraved on it together.

He says I have to go through my stuff again. "You can't bring more than three," he says, and he's firm on this point, resolute with arms folded.

And he's right. I can't. Because our car is little, and we don't have the money to ship anything, and even if we did, the new apartment is tiny. So I get down on my knees and start sifting through my life again, even though I know already that I won't find anything else I can part with, just like I didn't the last time I looked through and the time before that. But life is all about compromise, so I empty each box item by item, and lay everything side by side on the floor and pick them up, inspect them one by one, just so he will know that I'm doing all I can.

My collection of Lobster Pals, almost complete, only missing Papa Lobster, who one winter was the most sought after Christmas gift. My World's Most Loved Children's Poetry book, with pages wrinkled and brown from the time I dropped it into a muddy pond. My first pair of lace up shoes, which, according to family legend, I spent almost three full hours tying and retying when I first got them, committing how to do it to memory. My little league uniform, which was in fact the whole reason I joined the team—because I wanted to wear what those kids were wearing.

I can't throw these things out. I can't give them away. They are part of me, or I am part of them, or we are irreversibly entangled with each other. At least we once were. And sometimes late at night, when the noise of the TV and the hum of the refrigerator aren't enough to drown out the sound of nothing, I like to believe that we still are. That I am still that little girl who assigned meaning to inanimate objects, who saved these things because she believed that they mattered.

But I don't have a choice.

And he is waiting.

"I just need a little more time," I say, looking up at him from my perch on the floor. "Can't I just have a little more time?"

He kneels down beside me and rests his hand on my shoulder, squeezes. And instead of answering my question, which I know is unanswerable because time is not his to grant, he asks me a question of his own. "Why do these things mean so much to you anyway?" When I don't answer his question, he piles another on top of it. "What good can come of clinging to your childhood?" Another unanswerable question.

I want to tell him that I'd like to believe that what we had when we were children we can still have when we grow older, that there are some things in life worth holding on to, but the words would sound hollow and I know they aren't true. So instead I say nothing, just wordlessly begin moving things into a pile that will fill up a box, and then another, and another—all of my boxes, every one but three—which, later today, I will donate to the thrift store downtown.

PART TWO:
PIRATES

THIS IS NOT A FAIRY TALE

Once upon a time there was a young girl who was haunted by the memory of her dead parents. Her name was Lucy, and she was poor and plain. She had that sort of red hair that's not really red but orange, and pale almost yellow skin to match. Her nose was long and pointed, and her eyebrows, which were several shades lighter than the orange of her hair, were almost invisible unless the light hit them in just the right way. Even when she was a baby, her parents used to look at her and say, "She'll have to work hard, this one. She won't be able to coast on her looks."

Poor Lucy's parents, they knew all about working hard. They owned a business that failed. A flower shop. Only the flowers in that shop were all wilted and dead. The shop was lit well, lots of windows, plenty of sunshine, and Lucy's parents were educated florists, both. They knew how much water to give and how many stems could fit into what sized vase. The shop was crammed with shelves and shelves of vases filled with roses, carnations, violets, chrysanthemums. Any flower you could want and many more besides. But the colors were all drained and the blossoms drooping. Brown edged its way down from the tip of each petal. And nobody wants to buy flowers like that.

Lucy's parents grew the flowers in their own garden out back. They fed them and sang to them and waited to clip them until the flowers were ready, but the second the flowers would enter the shop, their colors would fade and their stems would turn down. Nobody knew why. There was nothing to do but watch the flowers die, one by one, and to watch Lucy's parents' dreams die along with them. You see, Lucy's parents had sunk every penny they had into that shop, and several that they didn't have, as well. When they finally had to admit failure, they were so deeply in debt that there was no hope but to burn down the shop, with themselves in it, and hope for a better life for their baby, Lucy. But it didn't work. Insurance fraud. It was obvious from the start.

And so Lucy went to live with her Gram and Gramps, who could barely afford to feed themselves but who took her in, anyway, because how could they possibly not? Lucy's Gram and Gramps lived on a farm. A farm that was dying, too, like Lucy's parents' flowers. But Gram and Gramps worked hard to keep the farm going, and they managed well enough. Gram and Gramps grew all manner of things on that farm. All kinds of vegetables that tasted just like vegetables. Which was precisely the problem. The plan had been to start a farm and sprinkle the earth with sugar and flavored waters, and to grow as a result a whole new kind of vegetable. Vegetables that small children wouldn't mind eating.

Gram and Gramps had saved money for years to buy the farm. A lifetime of hard work only to quit their jobs and work even harder. But they had believed it would be worth it to make the world a sweeter place, and it probably would have been, had their plan to sugar the earth worked. But it hadn't. The sugar threw everything off balance, and the plants could hardly take root. And even when Gram and Gramps gave up on the idea, just decided to run a regular old farm, it seemed the damage had been done. Their crops were weak and underdeveloped, when they turned out at all. But even though times were hard, they took Lucy in when she needed a home.

They didn't want Lucy to forget her parents, who had loved her so much that they let their bodies burn so that Lucy might know something better than wilted flowers, so Gramps put a picture of Lucy's parents on her bedside table. The frame was wooden and peeling, and Lucy got splinters the few times she tried to pick it up. There had been a crack in the glass so Gramps had taken it off, and the photo, perhaps from age or from exposure to the humid farmhouse air, had begun to bow out in the center, held in place by the frame on its top and bottom. It looked like the picture was trying to escape.

The image itself, the only image Lucy would ever know of her parents, had been taken with a cheap camera and the film had been overexposed. Lucy's parents' skin was too white against their black clothes, and their eyes blazed red from the intensity of the camera's flash. And their smiles, which were warped on one side each where they pressed their cheeks together, were too big and too deliberate to be genuine. Lucy thought they looked like they were taunting her. Like they wanted to remind her again and again that they would break free of this frame eventually and once they did there would be nothing to protect her.

But Gram and Gramps didn't know that the picture frightened Lucy and so every night after the chores were done, Gram would tuck Lucy in and kiss her on the cheek and tell her a story about her mother. "When your mom was just a girl," Gram would say, "she insisted I buy her a fluffy white cat. She named him Kindness and brought him with her everywhere. Thought he would keep the witches away."

And Lucy would look at the picture on her nightstand, her mom and her dad with gaping smiles and eyes glowing red, and Lucy would think, they're dead. Their bodies were engulfed in flames and they're dead. And Lucy would wonder if Kindness had worked, or if her mom was a witch now, or a ghost.

And after Gram would kiss Lucy on the forehead, turn out the light, and close her bedroom door, Lucy would pull the blanket over her head and wait for the nightmares to come. Her parents came to her every night as a witch and a warlock wanting to claim her soul. Sometimes they would tear at her, pull her legs and drag her into the ground. Other times they would swoop around her, pecking and clawing like vultures. And sometimes they would just sit, their grotesque smiles and glowing eyes trained on their daughter, and they would stare until Lucy couldn't take it anymore, and she would scream herself awake. That was how she always woke up. No matter the nightmare, Lucy always woke up tangled in the sheets and screaming to a dark, empty room.

Gram and Gramps, who were growing old already and whose hearing had never been great to begin with, didn't know about Lucy's nightmares, so they never thought to ask her about them, or comfort her, or take the picture away. And Lucy, who was nothing if not grateful for all that her grandparents had done for her, never said anything about it.

Well, Lucy grew to be tall and trim, strong and healthy, too. Her skin darkened a shade or two—still pale, but a glowing sort of pale—from working long days out in the sun, and her muscles grew taut and firm. And one day, when Lucy was nineteen, she met the man that would be her knight in shining armor. His name was Stephen, and even if he had lived in the days of knights and chivalry, he likely would have been a traveling bard or some equally ineffectual thing. The sort to sing the songs about the heroes. Stephen was twenty-two and he was hired on to help with the harvest that year. He was a high school dropout, traveled around doing this job and that, and he took his guitar everywhere he went, slung on a strap on his back.

When Stephen saw Lucy, his first thought was how plain she was and how sad it must be, to be so plain. Stephen was quite handsome, as I'm sure you've already guessed, with his sleek black hair and his firm tanned skin and his slender guitarist's fingers. So his first thought was that Lucy was inordinately plain, but his second thought, when he put his hoe down and stepped up to Lucy to introduce himself, was that she had sad eyes. Passionate eyes. There was such loss and pain and perseverance in those green eyes, they were almost beautiful.

When he introduced himself he felt awkward. A new feeling. Girls were one thing Stephen was not afraid of. There was no reason a girl should leave him feeling so hesitant, and especially a girl as plain as Lucy. "My name's Stephen," he said to her and then rubbed the palm of his right hand on his pants to wipe it clean before reaching out to shake her hand.

Lucy, who knew she was plain and who knew, too, that a man as handsome as Stephen could never be interested in someone like her, didn't stop to think about how best to win over this dark haired stranger. Instead, she looked down at his sweating palm with disgust. "I'd rather not," she told him. "Sorry, but I'd rather not."

Stephen looked down at his own hand, realizing for the first time that it was more than simply sweaty, it was grimy and brown, streaked black underneath the fingernails. The skin, he noticed, was rough and dry and almost a ghostly white in the creases. Dirt had seeped underneath the dry patches and remained caught there, unreachable by soap.

He pulled his hand back and laughed nervously. "Sorry about that," he said. He tried not to show the shock on his face that a girl would not want to touch him. Would be repulsed by him. Nothing like this had ever happened before. "Anyway," he said, "my name's Stephen. I'm the new farmhand."

Lucy nodded and said, "I'm Lucy." And then she walked away.

The rest of the day as Stephen worked in the fields he kept noticing his hands, how dirty they were, and worn. How obvious it was what line of work he was in. Nobody had ever looked at him, really looked, before.

That evening at dinner he laid his hands palm up on the table and stared into the calluses and the cracks. He wondered how he could have never noticed before how ugly his hands were and thought about all the women whose soft skin he had handled with these coarse hands. They had never, not one of them, mentioned it to him.

Gramps saw him looking and motioned his fork at Stephen's hands. "Your hands bothering you, son?"

Stephen dropped one hand to his lap and used the other to pick up his fork and stab at his casserole. "I guess so, sir. A little."

Gramps grunted and asked, "Did you break 'em open or something?"

Stephen shook his head. "No, sir."

Gramps eyed Stephen's right hand as Stephen moved the fork to his lips. "Strong working hands, you've got," he said. "The hands of a man, not a boy."

Stephen nodded and glanced at Lucy, who didn't say anything, just ate quietly and kept her green eyes turned down.

Gram and Gramps gave Stephen the room next to Lucy's and he stayed up late that first night, strumming his guitar with his rough and dirty fingers and singing into the adjoining wall. He didn't know why, but he hoped that the plain girl with the sad eyes would take notice of his plain, sad song. It was a sort of thank you, he supposed, and an apology, too, for noticing her homeliness first before her eyes.

Lucy sat with her ear pressed against the other side of the wall and wished that the handsome man with the dirty hands and the simple song would keep playing forever so she wouldn't have to sleep. But eventually, Stephen's eyelids grew heavy and he rested his guitar on his lap and his head against the wall, and drifted into a doze. And Lucy, no matter how hard she fought it, fell asleep too, her head resting on her side of the wall.

In the middle of the night, Stephen was awakened by the most horrible screams. Frantic and urgent. The girl in the other room was gasping and moaning and crying for help. She was choking on the very air she breathed. Stephen jumped to his feet, letting his guitar clatter to the wood floor, and rushed out of his room and into Lucy's. He flicked on the light and stood with muscles tensed and stance ready to fight.

Lucy looked up at him from her position on the floor, green eyes glistening with tears. There was no one in the room but herself. There had never been anyone hurting her but herself.

Stephen stepped forward and reached out to help the dazed girl to her feet.

She took his hand, in spite of its roughness, and let him heft her up. He led her to her bed and laid her down and folded the blankets tightly around her. "What were you dreaming about?" he asked.

Lucy thought about lying, but she decided that telling the truth at last would be a release. So she said, "Flowers. Burning flowers and my parents, who are dead." She looked up at Stephen and waited for him to react.

He shrugged, because he didn't know what she meant, and said, "I'm sorry to hear that." Because that's what you're supposed to say when someone tells you someone else is dead.

"It's okay," she said. "They died when I was a baby. I never knew them." And then she closed her eyes. Just once she wanted to fall asleep with another person in the room.

The next morning Lucy opened her eyes feeling rested and at peace. And then she remembered why and for a moment she thought she would be sick. She felt for reasons she could not understand herself that this hired boy, an utter stranger, somehow knew her in a way deeper and more complete than her own Gram and Gramps did.

But that was nonsense. He had simply walked in on her having a nightmare. That was all. People have nightmares, Lucy reminded herself. They mean nothing. She glanced at the picture—at her mother and her father and their demon eyes—and then clucked her tongue. Nightmares mean nothing at all.

Lucy dressed and hurried out into the field, where she found Stephen leaning against a wooden post. When he saw her approaching from the direction of the farmhouse, Stephen straightened up and blushed in spite of himself. He dropped his hands to his sides, then folded them into each other, then laid one against the post and plunged the other into his pocket.

You see, he felt ashamed of what had happened just as Lucy did, for he felt that he had done her some unspeakable wrong. He had stayed gazing down at her in her bedroom long after her breathing had steadied and she was clearly fast asleep. He had thought how charming she was in the dim light. In spite of her pale skin and orange hair, she had almost looked beautiful. Her lips had looked so soft that an urge had taken him. He had brushed his thumb across her lips, from one corner of her mouth to the other, before he realized how inappropriate that was, how inexcusable. How disgusted she would be to know that he had touched her mouth with his filthy hand.

He hadn't slept at all the rest of the night. Stayed up tossing and turning and wondering whether or not she might actually have been awake still, might actually have felt his thumb brushing tenderly against her lips. And now here she was, walking toward him with a look of stern determination.

Lucy had meant to thank Stephen. She had made up her mind that she would apologize, try and explain herself a little, and then she would ask him please not to mention it to her grandparents. "It might worry them," she had planned to say. "And it's really nothing serious." But when she walked up and found the hired boy shifting his hands from place to place, doggedly trying to remind her, she felt certain, of her refusal to touch his hand the day before, her heart hardened against Stephen and she said, "My grandparents don't pay you to stand around doing nothing."

Stephen blushed even deeper. So she had been awake. "Sorry," he said and rushed back to his work, grateful that she at least hadn't mentioned his indiscretion. He was certain he could keep hold of himself in the future, but he couldn't bear the thought of her asking him about it, of having to explain to her how it made him feel—being given the opportunity to be a hero so suddenly and unexpectedly—and of how she made him feel, too, anxious and unsure of himself.

That night, Stephen was awakened again by the sound of Lucy's shrieks. Even though he had told himself he wouldn't go to her if it happened again—he was, of course, afraid he might lose himself and feel the need to touch her soft skin once more—the intensity of her screams was too much for him to take. He rushed into her bedroom, turned on her light, and shook her gently awake.

She stared up at him at first with eyes dull and afraid, but when her eyes became clear, they moistened and overflowed. She was so ashamed of herself for having woken him again, and even more ashamed for having thought such cruel things about him earlier. "I'm so sorry," she said groggily as Stephen picked up the blanket, which she had kicked onto the floor, and laid it over her shivering body.

Now as you can imagine, Stephen didn't know what Lucy was sorry about, but it didn't matter because either way, he would have given her the same quiet response: "Don't be."

Closing her eyes, Lucy sighed and let her body sink back into the mattress. Stephen stood up to leave. Lucy heard the rustle of his pajama bottoms as his legs straightened, and her eyes flitted open again. She called to him, "Stephen?"

He looked down at her half-asleep green eyes, and it took every ounce of willpower he had to keep himself from brushing his fingers against her smooth forehead. "Yes?"

"Will you stay with me?" She yawned. "Until I fall asleep?"

Stephen felt that he had been given a great honor in her asking, but he worried that he might forget himself again if he was allowed to linger and admire her simple, sleeping almost-beauty. So he shook his head, told her, "I'd better not," and before she could protest he stepped out of her room and closed the door behind him.

The next night and the next and the night after that, Lucy woke Stephen up again with her unbridled terror. Each time, he rushed to her side and tucked her back into her bed, but he always left quickly while she was still awake. Lucy understood his hesitancy at staying until she fell asleep as part punishment for the pitiless heart she had turned to him those first two days and part aversion to her homely face. He must be afraid she would get the wrong idea. She understood his caution, but still each night she silently hoped he would stay there by her side until she fell asleep.

During the days, as Lucy went about her work on the farm, she would think of the nights and imagine what might happen if she asked Stephen to stay with her. But her fantasies never failed to leave her feeling ashamed because no matter how the different scenarios unfolded in Lucy's mind, they all came to the same end: he would reject her again.

But after the fifth night, Lucy sought Stephen out in the fields anyway. "I have an idea," she told him. "I want to see if it'll work."

"Okay," he said and leaned on his shovel.

132

"I was wondering if," she said and cleared her throat, scratched her head. "That is, if you don't think you would feel too uncomfortable, or, anyway, if you think it wouldn't be too much of a burden . . ." She stopped and almost resolved to give up on the whole thing, but the way he was looking into her eyes, she could never explain it but she felt right then as though he didn't have it in him to deny her a request. "Do you think you might sleep in my room tonight?"

As you know, Stephen had reservations, but Lucy was right: Stephen could deny her nothing as long as she held him in her solemn gaze. Such earnest despair shone out of those eyes. This was her only hope, he could tell, and he couldn't—or at least wouldn't—say no. So on the sixth night, Stephen lay on the floor beside Lucy's bed, singing softly to her and holding her pale hand in his rough, dirty one until she fell asleep.

But the nightmares, they still came.

At first Lucy thought she was still awake—she was resting in her bed holding Stephen's hand—but the air in the room was heavier than usual, thick, and the hand in her hand wasn't rough like Stephen's. It was smooth and hard like glass. Lucy lifted her hand up, bringing the other hand with it, and saw the long pointed fingernails, tainted crimson with what appeared to be dried blood, and she knew that it wasn't Stephen's hand, but her mother's.

This time it was only a low moan, soft enough that Stephen probably wouldn't have heard it if he had been in his own room. But he hadn't been. He had been fast asleep on Lucy's floor, and the mewling sound that bubbled up from deep inside her throat woke him right away. Stephen sprang to his feet, turned on the light and then shook Lucy awake. Her eyes lulled open, already crisp and aware. For a moment they stared at each other, neither wanting to be the one to say it first. That it had failed, Lucy's plan. That Stephen had failed her. You see, Lucy believed, and Stephen did too, that Stephen's presence would make the nightmares go away. That all she had ever really needed was her true hero by her side. If the nightmares came either way, it meant that Stephen must not be the one.

After what felt like an eternity, Stephen said to Lucy, "I guess I'll go back to my room."

Lucy didn't say anything, just rolled over on her side and tried to keep the tears inside until she heard the door clasp shut.

On the seventh night and the eighth and the ninth, Stephen slept in his own bed and ignored the screams when they drifted through the wall. It was hard because he felt so sorry for Lucy, the poor plain girl with such sadness in her eyes. He wanted so badly to rush to her, even though he knew he could do her no good. But it was better for her this way, he told himself. Better for her to wait for the one who might save her.

On the seventh night he had to press his pillow to his ears to dull the sound. It wasn't the noise itself that bothered him, but the realization that he wasn't the hero he had begun to believe himself to be. The eighth night he stayed up all night strumming his guitar, and the ninth he began to plan where he would go next—because he hadn't slept in two days and would surely not sleep again until he left this haunted place.

That night he pulled out his map, dirty and tattered from years of perpetual use, and unfolded it and flattened it against the wooden floor. He tried to smooth its creases with the palms of his hands, but his jagged dry skin caught the folds, created even deeper wrinkles. He pulled his hands up and held them before his face, stared into the dead white skin and the dirt caught underneath it, the deep wrinkles that would endure, he knew, forever and ever and ever after that. So like the ragged old map, these hands. A map of where he'd been. He tried to find the deepest crease, the crease that the crooks at the fair would call his lifeline, and he wondered whether these hands had to be a map of where he was going, too.

134

During those long, lonely nights, Lucy hardly slept at all. Her first night alone again, the nightmares were so much fiercer than they had been the past few nights, and the next night they were fiercer still. By Lucy's third night alone she had to all but physically restrain herself from rushing into Stephen's room and pleading with him to stay with her again, or at least let her curl up in a ball at the foot of his bed.

In the daytime, Stephen and Lucy both walked around like images of the living dead, though they wouldn't have known it because they were avoiding each other. The deepening circles underneath their eyes didn't alarm Gram and Gramps so much as the lumbering way both Stephen and Lucy walked and the dull emptiness that gaped out of their eyes. Gram was convinced they were ill with something catching, but Gramps thought it was the pains of thwarted and thwarting love. Neither suspected the truth: that their dear Lucy had a curse that poor Stephen was helpless to lift.

The morning after the ninth night—the night Stephen sat awake planning his escape—Lucy stood in the kitchen washing the breakfast dishes. She saw movement in her peripheral vision, somebody in the doorway. When she turned to see who it was, the dish she had been scrubbing slipped from her fingers and broke into three neat pieces on the floor. It was her mother, but she was older now. Her mother if she hadn't burnt up in the fire.

"Lucy?" The woman took a step forward and Lucy flinched. "Dear?"

Lucy looked down at the three pieces of plate on the floor. Smooth white porcelain in clean lines at the edges—so beautiful, this unpainted white, and it was only visible because the plate had cracked.

Gram took another step forward and kneeled down to pick up the broken plate. "Are you alright, dear? Why don't you go lie down?"

Lucy nodded and left the room, but she didn't walk down the hall and into her bedroom. Instead, Lucy went to Stephen, found him in the cornfields amid the giant stalks, and begged him to reconsider.

He looked into her eyes, but looked away before they sucked him in. He shook his head. "I can't help you, Lucy. I wish I could but I can't."

"Nobody can," Lucy said. "Nobody's ever come close but you. Nobody's ever even noticed before."

Stephen looked down at his hands, curled them into fists, and then looked back up at Lucy. "I know what you mean."

Lucy reached out and took Stephen's hands, one in each of her own, much softer, cleaner hands. She didn't even shudder at his touch, he noticed. She didn't even seem to mind. "You can't make them go away," she said. "But they're much worse when you're not there."

Stephen thought back to the moans from that first night, and then the next and then the next. They had seemed to get better, and the time he stayed all night in Lucy's room they had been the mildest yet. It just hadn't been the dramatic change he had expected. And then when he had left again, turned a deaf ear or at least pretended to, they had suddenly seemed so much more severe. He squeezed her hands in his own and nodded. "Okay."

So he came to her again that night, and then the next, and the next after that. And the nightmares improved, though they never went away. Stephen and Lucy grew fond of each other, and eventually, as you already knew they would, Stephen and Lucy fell in love. Only it wasn't the immediate kind of love that Lucy had been expecting, nor the heart-squeezing kind that Stephen had been so used to. It was a calmer sort of love, subdued and careful. The sort that loves you though you're plain for the sadness in your eyes or in spite of your work-worn hands for the beauty in your song.

And one day, many years later, Lucy and Stephen were married, and they all lived in the farmhouse together—Gram and Gramps and Stephen and Lucy and the red eyed picture of Lucy's parents. And Stephen and Lucy lived happily ever after, or at least they were mostly happy most of the time, which is enough, it turns out. Which is all you really need.

WHAT IF YOU MARRIED THAT GUY?

So, what if you married that guy? The one from high school who had the eyes so blue or green or brown, whatever it was, whose name you used to write over and over in your notebook, coupling it with your own, or writing before it Mrs. and Madame and the wife of? How different would your life be now, do you think? How much of a difference would that one small change have made?

Let's say you got up the courage to ask him out that time, you remember, when you had plotted out that elaborate plan, how you would call him or run into him somewhere and casually bring up the fact that you didn't have a date for the dance or that you always found Valentine's Day depressing. Or better yet, let's say he asked you out some time, to the big dance, maybe. The one you had held off on finding a date for because you were secretly hoping he would come around, and then when he didn't, you spent the night at home watching reruns with your parents or playing board games with your kid sister.

Picture it.

You're standing in front of the mirror and admiring yourself in your new dress or decent looking hand-me down, whichever. And he picks you up and you dance and he introduces you to all his friends and gets you punch and you both have a fantastic time. It's exactly like you thought it would be; he's just as sweet and understanding, asking questions about your personal life and your family and leaning in to listen to your answers, or else he's tough and disaffected, like you always wished you could be, and says, "Fuck the teachers and fuck the other students and fuck your parents and fuck this song," and you want so badly for him to fuck you.

That night with him is something completely new. And not because you've never had a date before—although back then maybe you hadn't, or if you had it had been with a boy you didn't really like, one who had taken you to a think film or ballroom dancing or to the zoo, and it had solidified in your mind that you would never have a chance with the sort of guy worth dating because you, you realized, weren't the kind of girl worth dating. But this experience is new for different reasons altogether. Reasons that would scare you if they didn't excite you so much. Reasons like how badly you want him to touch you, or how much you want his tongue in your mouth, or how much you would do anything, anything, if he would just tell you that you look pretty tonight.

In fact you fish for it, don't you? You hint around, make jokes and lean forward so he can get a good look down the top of your dress, try and let him know without actually coming out and saying it that you are that kind of girl, at least you will be with him if he just lets you know he wants you. But maybe he averts his eyes when you lean forward, and he changes the subject when you make those sultry quips. Maybe at the end of the night he just kisses you, a peck, really, and not even full on the mouth but on the corner, like he can't decide between your cheek and your lips and so hits neither.

But let's say just before he lets you out of the car, just when you're about to run up to your room, flop onto your bed and cry tears that will mix with your makeup and leave a permanent stain on your pillowcase, he asks you out for real. Asks you to be his girlfriend. And you forget, for a while, the pain of your rejected intimations. You forget what they told you in sex ed, that boys want to have sex with any girl they find attractive, because you're so giddy that you'll be his girlfriend now. That everybody will know it and they'll all look at you differently.

And so the next Monday at school he holds your hand and carries your books and tells you jokes, and you hold his hand back and let him open doors for you and fake laugh when he burps or makes fun of the out crowd. But maybe you used to be part of the out crowd, before he reached out and pulled you up the social ladder. Or maybe you weren't part of any crowd but you don't really think those jokes are funny. But you want him to like you, or keep liking you, and you like the fact that people are starting to notice you now as you walk down the hallways with his arm around you. And you like knowing that when you stay home sick, people will ask him where you are, and when he ditches school, people will ask you to pass messages on to him.

We'll assume that things keep going well and you eventually make it to prom. And maybe at prom he surprises you with a red rose corsage and also with a hotel room. You pretend to be surprised, a little unsure and maybe even offended. But before he backs down, which you can see in his eyes he will do very easily, you slip your hand into his and whisper, "Yes," in a way that you hope is very seductive.

It's all very fumbling and hesitant and it's over too quickly, which you choose to take as a sign of how sexy you really are. You have sex in the dark so it isn't until much later that you can actually say you've seen a naked man, but it doesn't matter because either way you're not a virgin anymore and he isn't, either, and you feel confident in assuming that people saw the two of you leave early and that they know why.

You end up pregnant, though, and even though you're sort of excited, you're probably afraid to tell him and even more afraid to tell your parents. But when you finally do let's say he astonishes you by proposing and your parents astonish you by begging you to have an abortion. You say yes to him and move out of your parents' house. You say you're going to go to community college next year, but for now, you'll have the baby and let him support you with his minimum wage job at the grocery store or his dad's hardware store or the video game store, where he doesn't have much of a future but he absolutely loves his job and isn't that more important?

But you can't really live off of his salary, and so you have to get a job, too. But you're also very pregnant and you feel tired and sick all the time and your ankles are swollen and your back is sore. He's always grumpy, too, so you end up not talking except to fight and not kissing except to fuck. But that's okay, really, because it's still him. It's you and him and everybody knows it. Nobody has to know that your belly looks like an overfilled balloon just about to pop, or that his penis looks like a raisin and smells like a decaying corpse.

Well, you have the kid and you put off going to college another year, and then two, and then indefinitely. Maybe he gets promoted at the grocery store or hardware store or video store; he makes manager and has a whole lot more responsibility for a little bit more pay. But he still isn't making enough for you not to have to work, so you have to stagger your work hours so that one of you is always home to take care of the baby.

Time passes and you learn how to make tamales or lasagna or curry because it's a tradition in his family. And you wash the dishes, too, and do most of the work with the kid, because he does work long hours, after all, and he's exhausted when he gets home. Plus he's always reminding you—or at least, he told you once and you assume it's always on his mind—how his mom used to get up at three in the morning so she could do the housework, make breakfast, and do her hair before going in to work. His dad, you assume, slept in, but you never ask.

And eventually he starts complaining that you've let yourself go. That's the way it feels, anyway. That's what he seems to be implying when he watches you plod across the kitchen in the mornings, pull out an entire carton of ice cream, and stand by the freezer shoveling it into your mouth in huge spoonfuls. You've gained some weight since high school and it doesn't look good on you, you'll be the first to admit. And you don't always wear makeup, unless you're going out, and half your wardrobe consists of jeans, and not the nice kind, because he won't let you buy the nice ones; they're too expensive. But none of this, you think silently to yourself, is your fault. You're not saying that it's his, no, certainly not. But it isn't yours, and you're positive that he believes that it is.

Somehow you get pregnant again, which is a surprise to both of you because you almost never have sex anymore, since he isn't really that attracted to you these days—you're sure of it—and you're too busy and tired to care. You're excited about telling him because you expect him to be happy, but he isn't and you actually feel ashamed. Not for being pregnant—though you're sure he probably believes that this, too, is somehow your fault—but for actually thinking that this would change anything.

He starts coming home later and later at night as your pregnancy wears on. You're gaining more weight this time around and you can just tell that he thinks you're overeating, even though your doctor says it's perfectly natural (you ask about it every single time you come in for a checkup). But anyway, you start suspecting that he's cheating and you're more embarrassed than hurt. You imagine him telling his mistress, who is probably younger and better looking than you both, that his wife is fat and stupid and you imagine both of them laughing at your expense.

You start paying extra close attention to his every move. Every excuse he gives for staying out late, you scrutinize. Every article of his clothing you thoroughly sniff before tossing it into the washing machine. You become obsessed with catching him. You want to humiliate him; you want him to plead for forgiveness. You have no intention of offering it, but you want to hear him beg. You want to reject him.

You start asking your kid if his daddy has mentioned another lady. Your kid doesn't know what you're talking about and thoughtlessly mentions it to him. He is outraged. He accuses you of snooping, of dragging your child into it, and of being a pathetic excuse for a wife. You glare at him but don't say anything. Let him have his say, you think to yourself. You'll find the proof soon enough.

You begin calling him at odd times during work, thinking that you'll find him inexplicably absent, but he's always there and you always hang up without saying anything. Determined to catch him in the act, you hire a babysitter one day and prowl around outside his work until you see him leave, pull his jacket close around him, and walk around the corner to a nearby café.

Giddily, you find a comfortable perch behind a bush and peer into the café window, watching as he orders a coffee and sits down at a table by himself. You start planning out what you will say to him when you confront him, whenever She shows up. How you will speak just loud enough so everyone in the café can hear but quiet enough so they won't write you off as hysterical. How you will push your extremely pregnant belly out even further, and midway through your teary accusation, you will lean against the table, as though you are about to pass out, as though just the thought of his affair is putting your unborn baby's life in danger.

You wait and wait and wait, but nobody shows up to meet him at the café. He just sits and stares into his coffee for an hour and then stands up, drops some change onto the table for a tip, and leaves. You know you should hurry home, that he will be home soon and he will talk to the babysitter and he will know what you have been up to. But you don't feel like dealing with it all yet so instead you walk down the street and find a diner and sit at the bar next to a handsome younger man with spiky black hair or smooth tan skin or heavily tattooed arms.

The man smiles at you and asks when you're due. Trying to be coy, you say, "Whenever you want me to be," and his eyebrows raise, his forehead wrinkles, and he doesn't say anything after that. He sits for another minute, staring down at his plate before he wordlessly picks it up and moves to a table at the other end of the diner.

You sit there for half an hour, determined to eat your scrambled eggs or pancakes or hashbrowns with dignity intact, but as soon as you force the last bite into your mouth, you pay your bill, leave an unreasonably large tip, and go back to your car, walking faster than you've ever walked in your life.

When you get home, he is waiting with his jacket on and his suitcase packed. He tells you he knows where you were, and he tells you that he's tired, so very tired. Much to your surprise, he leaves you, and now you're alone with his child and his unborn baby on the way.

You don't hear anything for several months. Then you hear from his lawyer that he wants a divorce. He is, you find out from a friend of a friend, already dating again and he will be fighting for custody once things settle down. In your desperation you start drinking, or eating a lot of chocolate, or watching soap operas. And you start thinking about all the things you could have done, who you could have been if he hadn't asked you to that dance all those years ago, or if you had just said no, in spite of how much you had wanted him to ask.

Back then, all you cared about was being the sort of girl that could get the sort of guy like him. It was so important to you to impress the other girls, to have that boyfriend they all wanted because he was handsome and popular and rich, or rugged and wild and dangerous, or smart and funny and had a real future ahead of him.

You should have known all along, you would be telling yourself right now if you had married that guy. Should have known that things would end up like this with a guy like that. Because you were always the smarter one, or maybe you weren't but you had more common sense. You could have gone on and done great things if he hadn't interrupted your life, held you back, pushed you down—you wouldn't know, of course, about what you did go on to do, wouldn't know this version of yourself that lies awake at night and wonders. But instead of those things you would be sure you could have become, you would have just become fat and angry and at the end of it all, alone. You would shake your head and you would sigh and you would tell yourself over and over again that you're not saying it's his fault but it certainly isn't yours. No, whoever's fault it is, it couldn't possibly be your own.

WISHING ON AIRPLANES

Professor Avram Philips met the one who turned out not to be the One on his way home from class on a February afternoon. He wouldn't have met her if he hadn't been walking home that day, lugging in his tan canvas bag a stack of papers and three books—two for class and one that he had borrowed from his wife. They were heavy volumes, too, all three, and it was cold. The dark clouds hanging in the sky threatened rain.

He hadn't been walking long, no more than half a mile, before the muscles in his back began to tighten and ache. He stopped to reposition his bag, but the slight reallocation of weight did no good. The strap of his bag felt like it was digging a permanent ridge into his shoulder blade. It had taken him by such surprise that morning, the news that he would have to walk home, that he hadn't really prepared himself for the journey. Not that he would have been well prepared otherwise. After all, it had been years since he had gone for a long walk. You don't just wake up one morning and decide you're going to walk two miles today, not if you aren't the walking type.

And to top it all off, class had been downright miserable that day. They had just stared at him, the handful of students who had actually shown up, that is. Forced him to blather off on tangents just to fill the damned silence. It was American Poetry, usually his favorite American Lit topic even though it wasn't specific enough, only worked as an undergrad class. But that spring he had been having a particularly lousy semester. The students were listless and unresponsive, and the poems he had selected were an exceptionally passionate set. How these students could read—or in many of their cases, he suspected, not read at all—these exact poems and not be moved was so far outside the realm of Professor Philips's comprehension he couldn't even wonder without feeling angry at the decay of America's youth, not to mention the American education system, which had done such a poor job of preparing these kids for college and, more importantly, for his class.

He hated to be one of those doddering old men, already and only age fifty-six. The type of man who did nothing but complain about how much better the world was when he was young. But it had been better back then, Philips was certain, and if his gray hair and ever loosening skin signified nothing else, they should at least count as badges of experience and wisdom. He was thinking about just that, the rapidly increasing signs of aging that covered his face, his body, his skin, when he heard the first pop and knew instantly that it had come from his left knee.

He stopped. Looked down. Glared down, really. Tried to stare the kneecap into submission. He took another step and heard another pop, felt his right knee jump slightly and then drop back into place. Another step, another pop. Step step step. Pop pop pop. Philips stopped again, this time to look around him, see if anyone nearby was hearing what he heard, was looking at him with concern or with pity. But he was alone on the sidewalk.

He grunted and took another step, heard another pop. It was his wife's fault that he'd had to walk home at all. She had taken the car that morning, even though the car was his, purchased with his professor's salary. But her unpainted but for the rust and primer truck (how fitting, he had always thought, that she should have such a truck) had broken down that morning, and in lieu of finding alternative arrangements to get to work herself, she had asked him, "Do you mind?" as she pulled his keys from the bowl on the counter. Of course he had damn well minded, especially since he had warned her about this very thing when she had insisted on buying the old truck. But she had said it would hold up well enough for her purposes.

She had given him a ride to campus that morning, and he had all but choked on the meaningless chatter that had filled the space between them. When she had dropped him off, asked him what time she should pick him up, he'd waved the idea off. Told her he'd walk, that he'd be glad for the exercise, just so he wouldn't have to endure the drive a second time. So now she was probably on her way home in his car with nothing in the seat beside her but a small leather handbag and that stupid black notebook she insisted on taking with her every day to work. As if there would ever be anything worth writing about at the daycare.

Meanwhile he was struggling with a heavy bag and rogue knees, and the sky was most certainly going to open up any minute. He heard a distant drum of thunder overhead and looked up, waited for the lightning flash, but it didn't come. He counted to himself, one one-thousand, two one-thousand, three. Nothing. He looked back at the sidewalk in front of him. Maybe it was supposed to be the other way around. See the flash of lightning, count, then hear the thunder. That didn't seem right, but suddenly he wasn't sure. Felt even a little embarrassed that he might have gotten it wrong.

Of course, it didn't matter either way. What difference did it make how far away the lightning was when the point was that a storm was definitely on its way. The point was he would have to take the bus. He hadn't wanted to take it at first because he wasn't that sort of person, the bus sort. Something felt uncomfortable, wrong, about a distinguished college professor riding home on public transit. But in addition to the imminent

148

rain, he shouldn't push these knees any further. There was a bus stop not far from his house, and though he didn't know which route he should take to get home, he was a college professor, after all. How difficult could it be to figure it out?

He picked up the pace to get to the nearest bus stop, and his knees kept right on popping with every step. He scowled. He couldn't remember growing old. In fact, he had always felt he looked too young and had spent most of his life longing for gray hair and a thick, Santa Claus like beard to make him look more distinguished, more the professor that he knew he had always been on the inside. And his wife, who had always looked, he thought, a little bit older than she should, had grown older, still. When he looked at the wrinkles around her eyes and noticed that opaque, dazed look that always seemed, now, to cover what was once sharp and alert, he saw the signs of his own aging body peering back at him. And she was only fifty, his wife. But in the twenty-two years since they had married, since she had graduated with her master's degree and they had been allowed to make it official, she had seemed to age more rapidly and with more intensity than Professor Philips would ever have imagined possible.

The nagging awareness that his was no grand romance, the sort he might read about in the poems his students thought a waste of time, only grew stronger as his wife aged beside him. It's no wonder, then, that the girl caught Professor Philips's eye as he drew near the bus stop. She was sitting on the bus stop bench, slender and pretty and oblivious to the world, and she was reading, Professor Philips noticed right away, his favorite contemporary American poet. Well, one of the top five, at least. She sat on the bench, legs crossed, with the book held up in front of her with her left hand, her right hand awkwardly suspended in the air and making notes in the margins.

He tried to steady his quaking knees as he approached the girl, whose eyebrows were so perfectly arched and whose lips

149

so mauve and puckered. He walked up to the bench slowly, his steps cautious and their accompanying pops dull and faint. He sat down beside her and rested his bulky canvas book bag at his feet. "He's great," he said, pointing at the front flap of her book and trying not to seem like he was trying.

He wasn't trying, he told himself; after all, he was a married man. No matter that the marriage was a sexless one, and good riddance for that, since his wife had gained enough weight throughout their twenty-two years of marriage to be entirely unappealing even to the least discerning of men. It wasn't a happy marriage, no, but that didn't mean he would throw himself at every girl he happened to see reading an interesting book. He was above such things, he told himself. He just wanted to meet the girl and perhaps discuss the poet's work, his grasp of language, his smooth interweaving of theme and implication.

She looked up, an uncomprehending stare in her shades of grey eyes. He motioned again to the front cover and she followed the line of his finger with her eyes. "Oh, yeah," she said, nodding noncommittally. "It's not bad so far."

She was young. Too young, he supposed. Young enough to be one of his students and that was a path he planned never again to tread. But she wasn't one of his students, and even though her dark brown hair was highlighted in shocking red streaks that couldn't possibly have been meant to look natural, even though a glittering blue ring was laced through the edge of her willowy left eyebrow, he thought she looked remarkably mature. Almost as though she were an older soul trapped inside a supple, youthful body.

And anyway, all he wanted was a conversation. "I teach his work sometimes in my Contemporary American Poetry class." He had thought perhaps the knowledge that he was a teacher, a college professor, might impress her. It would have done him when he was her age and avidly devouring every poet he could get his hands on.

But she barely seemed to notice his declaration. "Mm," she said, not even looking up from the book. She made another quick scribble in the margins.

He wondered if she thought he was too old, or at least, old enough to not be interesting anymore. But the other option, the idea that perhaps her lack of interest had nothing to do with him—that maybe she was simply so involved in the beautiful play of words before her that she couldn't tear herself free, not even for a moment, not even for the sake of politeness—was too tantalizing to ignore. He almost shuddered in pleasure at the very thought that this might be, yes, probably was why she was still sitting there reading, perfectly proportioned nose sunk deeply into the pages. And that was when he knew. This was it, at last. She was the One.

He didn't feel guilty for this new awareness. His wife was most certainly not the One, could never have been, and he couldn't, in truth, recall why he had married her at all. She was unattractive, and though he noticed it more the older she got, he couldn't remember ever having found her attractive. He supposed when he was young, in his early thirties and a new professor ready to go out and change the world, he had been unconcerned about his future wife's appearance. He had liked her; that was all. She was smart—an intellectual, and fond of poetry, too. And he had never been a shallow man, certainly not.

She used to write lousy poems that she would read aloud to him in bed, an anxious look of expectation on her face as she watched for him to nod or smile or close his eyes and bob his head to the cadence of each emphasized word. And while his reactions were always forced and her poetry terrible, there had been a certain tenderness to those moments that he had believed, once, could carry them through.

But as time went by and ten years bled into twenty and on to twenty-two, the things that didn't used to matter had begun to stack up, to build a wall between the two of them, severing any connection they might once have shared. She stopped writing poetry, and he hadn't complained because she had never really had much of a talent for it, anyway. And he stopped sharing with her the poems he loved—the ones he shared with his students and the ones he didn't.

It was a mistake, he had been thinking more and more lately, to marry the wrong person, to not wait for the right one. The problem had been he hadn't believed, in his youth, that there was a right person, not for him. Never, in all his life, had he found a kindred spirit; never had he been able to connect. There was no one in all the world, as far as Professor Philips could see, that he could talk to, just have a damned conversation with. Even so, he realized now, you can't just go marrying the first person that knocks on your door, and you can't get married in your thirties simply because time seems to be running out. He didn't remember having thought of it in those terms at the time, all those years ago when he had proposed, but it seemed blatantly clear now that a lack of infinite time had been the cause of it all. Lack of time and hope, the two.

But here, now, was a second chance. A do-over. And he meant to grab hold of it and never look back. He coughed and shifted his weight around on the bench.

The girl didn't seem to notice.

He rummaged in his book bag, pulled out a red pen and a disorderly stack of essays. He pulled the top set of crookedly stapled pages from the stack and tried to read, but he couldn't concentrate, couldn't help but let his mind and eyes wander to the vision of beauty sitting next to him. He placed the essay back onto the stack and stretched his back dramatically. "Might even teach him this semester," he said.

"Hmm?" She looked up this time, but she didn't look interested. She looked confused and maybe even a bit irritated.

He pointed at her book again. "I teach American Lit over at the university."

Her slender eyebrows tilted in towards each other.

"Might teach that exact book this semester. Haven't decided." Of course, he had decided, well before the semester had begun. He had no intention of teaching this or any other book by the same author. But the words had just flown out of his mouth, seemingly of their own accord, and now he would seem crazy if he tried to take them back.

"Oh." She shrugged. "Awesome." It was such a cute word, awesome, coming from her. It was as though she was trying to be her age, trying to speak in the slang of a generation she probably had never quite fit in with. Too smart. Too bookish and independent. Surely she had been waiting her entire life for someone like him to come along.

Just as he had been waiting for her. He had seemed to develop less in common with his wife the longer they'd been married. Now they could hardly do anything together, didn't even watch movies together, or eat dinner. She didn't like onions and onions were his favorite. He was allergic to garlic and she drenched everything she ate in garlic powder. She had taken to making two separate meals, one for herself, onion free and garlic packed, and another for him, though his, he believed, she spent less time on, didn't put as much effort into, since she didn't like chopping onions and she wasn't going to eat it herself. And somehow everything, lately, had seemed to boil down to the difference between garlic and onions, to making two meals for two very different people.

"Do you go to the university?" he asked the girl.

"Nope." Her voice was curt and even a little disdainful.

Professor Philips hesitated. "Already graduated?" he asked cautiously.

"Never went, never intend to go," she said. "Waste of time and money. No offense." She waved her hand over the professor's stack of ungraded essays.

"No offense taken," he said and tried to smile encouragingly. He assumed she must have had bad teachers in high school, had never felt challenged. Had probably always made straight A's without even trying. As a result, she probably assumed that education was a joke. "I can see your point."

Her furrowed brow reminded him that she hadn't made a point, actually, had simply stated her disapproval of the very same institution he had devoted his entire life to, and she had done it without offering any reason or explanation. But that was the beauty of it, wasn't it? That she didn't have to. He understood.

The rumble of an approaching bus startled them both. Professor Philips watched, his palms beginning to sweat, as the girl stood up, closed her pen inside her book and folded the book under her arm. He stood, too, though he had no idea whether this was his bus. He leaned down, pulled his canvas bag onto the bench and tossed the stack of essays beside it.

"You might be interested in," he said, rummaging through the bag, "in this one here." He pulled out a battered blue hardcover with no dust jacket.

"What?" she asked, glancing back at him.

"I just thought you might like this one too." He held the book out to her and she looked down at it.

"Okay," she said. "Yeah, maybe I'll check it out." She tilted her head and squinted at the spine, reading, or pretending to read, the title and the author's name.

"You can borrow it," he said and pulled it back again.

"Huh?" she asked, glancing at the bus, which was almost there; she was almost gone.

154

He pulled the cap off of his red pen with his teeth and scribbled his name and office phone inside the book's front cover. "You can borrow it," he said, teeth clamped around the pen cap. He slid the pen between his teeth, popping the cap back on, and then dropped it on the stack of papers. "Go ahead. You can call me when you've finished with it." He held the book out to her.

She didn't reach out.

"I mean, to return the book, of course. That's why you'd want to call me," he said.

She stared down at the book. The bus pulled to a stop behind her, its brakes screeching. For a moment he thought she would refuse, just turn around and hop on the bus and leave him behind forever. But she didn't. She slowly reached out and accepted the book from him. "Thanks," she said and though her voice sounded uncertain, her words careful and pronounced, he felt that he had won her over at last.

She turned and climbed on the bus and Professor Philips turned back to the bench, collected his papers, his christened red pen, and tumbled them into his canvas bag. He would walk home, after all. His knees would hold—in fact, he was feeling surprisingly sprightly all of the sudden—and he saw no point in wasting such a delightful afternoon. The gray skies were pretty, after all, and the crisp chill to the wind had a refreshing edge to it.

When he got home he almost considered telling his wife then and there that it was over; he had found the One and didn't feel like pretending anymore. But something stopped him, a flash in her eyes that reminded him that she was human, too. That it would hurt. He didn't love her, didn't believe he had ever loved her, but he didn't want to hurt her unless he had to. So he stayed himself, made a flimsy excuse to go to bed early, where he could lie awake and stroke himself and dream about the girl he would no doubt be lying next to soon.

For the next several weeks, the professor found excuses to stay late at the office, to go in early and stick around through lunch. He checked his messages regularly and jumped, heart thumping unsteadily in his chest, every time the phone rang. But it was never her. It would always be some student or other, complaining about a grade or an assignment or offering an excuse for why they would be missing class that day. It was never the girl, and as the days continued on it became clear that she would not be calling. Nor would she be returning his book. He began to feel embarrassed and even a little ashamed, though not precisely about the fact that he was a married man, and a married man, most people would say, should know better. He was embarrassed about the thought that he might have messed it all up, somehow. Ruined his second chance.

He shouldn't have been so forceful, he told himself. Probably scared her away; she probably didn't even read the book because it made her too uncomfortable, this strange older man and his peculiar, inappropriate behavior. But you didn't win battles by staying home in bed, and he couldn't regret at least having tried. He regretted failing, of course, but he would never regret having tried.

But sooner or later, he had to admit defeat and he knew he would have to replace the book. After all, the book didn't really belong to him. It was his wife's, and even if it had been his, he would have wanted to replace it anyway, if only to show that he hadn't really lost anything at all. He went to his favorite used bookstore, the only one that was worth going to in town, to search for a cheap replacement copy after class one day. As he wandered down the quiet solitary aisles—so like the pews at a church, he always felt, but more meaningful—he thought about the girl and the book and the loss of something he had never had to begin with.

The girl had been pretty, yes, and most definitely intelligent, but that wasn't the reason why he had been so quick to consider her a prospect for his affections. It was more that the dullness in his wife's once keen eyes hadn't changed anything. Because things hadn't been so great to begin with. There had never been any romance between the two of them. There never could be. And while he had always, on some level, been aware of this, he hadn't, when he had decided to marry her all those years ago, considered it a problem. They had gotten along well, and he had believed that would be enough to sustain a fruitful marriage.

But he had been wrong, and it hadn't taken long before her habits, her unfailing consistency, started to get to him. Emerson was right about consistency, he thought. Small minds and all that. The way she owned something like ten pairs of the same black sneakers because she wanted to always have a replacement ready when her current pair, which she wore regardless of the outfit or occasion, had worn out. And the daycare, that barely above menial labor job that she continued to work at, even after she had gotten an advanced degree in literature, even though she knew full well it was an embarrassment to him.

He cringed to think about it. About the get-togethers, the faculty potlucks and dinner parties where the question would arise again and again: "What is it, Philips, that your wife does again?" In the early days of their marriage it had been an easy enough question to dodge. "Well she just graduated with her master's degree, of course. I'm sure she'll either find work as a lecturer or get her PhD soon."

But as time went on, it became increasingly more unavoidable that she had no intention of doing either, that she liked working at the daycare and meant to keep at it until retirement. Philips would find himself steering conversations with other faculty members this way and that, doing anything in his power to avoid the question. And he would leave her at home whenever possible. Conveniently forget to mention the invite, or assure her it would be a stuffy work affair and that the entire evening would be spent discussing curriculum and committees. She could come if she wanted, but he wouldn't be offended if she'd rather not.

He reached the poetry section, small but still the largest of any bookstore he had ever been to, and scanned through the spines until he came to the right book. They had only one copy, a battered old blue hardcover with no dust jacket, and he knew the moment he saw it, before he even pulled it from the shelf, that it had been his, once. Or his wife's, anyway. It was the very same copy he had given to the girl.

The girl was not so mature after all, he told himself as he flipped the cover open and stared down at his own name and office phone number harassing him in red ink. She had stolen the book, in a way. He had made it very clear that he was only lending it to her and she had traded it in, made a profit off the whole deal, though in all fairness, probably very little. He thought about marching to the front and demanding that they give him the book for free. He would show them his ID, his business card with the same name and number printed in neatly set letters, and reprimand them for not being more careful with their trades. But that wouldn't solve anything, would just embarrass him further, for one, and it wasn't really anybody's fault.

He bought the book and carried it home under his arm, devising an excuse to give his wife that might explain why his name and number were inside the book's cover. But he knew she probably wouldn't even wonder. Might not even notice, and if she did, she wouldn't say anything. It wouldn't occur to her to ask. When he walked inside, she was already in the kitchen preparing his dinner, which he would probably eat in the den so he could get some work done, or at least be alone for a bit. So he could hear himself think or maybe so he could not have to think, just be left alone and let his roaming mind sit still and quiet for a while. He could hear the water boiling through the open doorway, and the sickly smell of garlic and onions mingling together drifted in from the kitchen. What a disgusting combination, he thought. Two smells that simply should not be together.

He let his body sink into the time softened cushions of the couch and pulled open the book's ragged blue cover. He riffled the pages beneath his fingertips, flipped through them, willing himself to be happy that he had gotten the book back. He flipped past a page with scrawling black words tightly enclosed in the margins. He flipped back and folded the page open on his lap, struggled to read the rapid scribbles beside the poem. "Last night I made a wish on what turned out to be an airplane," the slanted writing said. "I thought it was my lucky star. But I was wrong."

He thought, with a flutter in his chest that he tried to tell himself was indigestion, that the note must be the girl's. What a delectably enigmatic thing to write in the margins. So she was a poet, then. He should have known.

He sat for a moment staring down at the note, letting the black ink dance before his eyes, letting it shift apart and then pull itself together again. There was something so familiar about the ink. No, not the ink. The writing. He had seen this handwriting before.

His stomach twisted inside him. The note, it was his wife's. And now that he looked at it, it wasn't so poetic after all. It was just the sort of nonsense she would come up with and think terribly deep and moving. What did she mean by it? Why would she think this worthy of writing down, in permanent ink, beside a poem, he recalled as he scanned through the printed words, about missing a train? Watching it pull from the station and deciding—yes here it was, at the end of the poem—not to chase it.

It seemed like such a waste of ink, a waste of time, too, and yet, clearly, it must have meant something to her. Enough to write it down, couple it forever with this poem about a train.

Funny that it had always been there, waiting in the margins for him to read. But he had never bothered to notice, never had the time.

"You in there, Ave?" his wife called from the kitchen.

He jumped and snapped the book closed, and then, as if hiding some evidence of guilt, he tossed it onto the table. "Yep," he said, standing up and stretching his arms, feeling his back pop on the right side, then on the left. Disparate pops, separate but collectively comforting, all the same.

"Dinner'll be ready in a sec." Her plump body appeared in the kitchen's doorframe. One arm wrapped around an oversized blue mixing bowl, she held a wooden spoon that dripped with white sauce. Her frizzy blonde hair was pulled back into a loose knot, and her blue eyes were red and puffy. From chopping onions, he supposed. Her nostrils were flared and her cheeks swollen and stained with the tears that had doubtless very recently trickled down them.

"Okay," he said.

She walked into the living room, her feet clothed in white ankle socks and padding on the carpet, and she sat down beside him on the arm of the couch. She rested the blue bowl on her lap and continued to stir. "How was your day?" she asked.

"Fine." His eyes darted to the book in front of them on the table. He thought that for sure she would see it there; she would see it and she would know.

But she didn't seem to notice its presence at all. May not, for all he knew, have ever noticed its absence. She just sat there stirring and stirring and chewing on her lip. She wasn't looking at him, either, just stared straight out at the wall on the other side of the room. "You'll get a kick out of this," she said at last. "Tommy, that one who looks like Dennis the Menace? He said the cutest thing today."

Philips grunted and looked at the wall, too.

160

"I asked him what he wanted to be when he grew up and he said a learned man." She shook her head and laughed but it was a strained laugh. More like an attempt at a chuckle than the real thing. "A learned man," she said. "A three-year-old boy. What a riot."

Philips nodded. "Hey, I've got some papers to grade." He stood up. "I'll be in the den," he said without looking at her.

She stood up, too. "Okay. I'll bring your dinner down when it's ready."

He nodded and walked down the stairs toward the den, thinking, still, about the margin note. Thinking that it seemed like such a waste of time, such an extraordinary waste of time.

NATURE

It was the blood—the warmth and taste of it in her mouth, the feel of it trickling down her throat—that kept coming back to Liz those first few days. The first night, when she woke up with the taste of blood in her mouth, she turned to see Toby's figure sleeping beside her. In the dim light of the moon, Toby's face was tinged blue, and his lips looked stiff. The beating of her heart drowned out any sound of breathing. She thought he was dead, and not only that but she thought he was the man, whose name she had refused to learn. It was only a moment, a split of a split of a split second, before she realized that he wasn't the man at all, he was Toby. He was dead Toby, and who do you think had killed him?

She got right up, even though it was only 1:30 in the morning. Got up and put on her robe, went to the kitchen to make some coffee and went out back to do some moonlit gardening singing softly to herself, la la la , trying to convince herself that she wasn't scared.

Part of the reason they had bought the house was for the giant backyard, for its gardening potential. She had never had much of a green thumb, as she had told Toby when they were deciding which of the four houses within their price range to buy, but she had always wanted to try, and she thought it would be a good way of bonding with their future children—there would be two, they had agreed. Ideally a boy and a girl, but you couldn't plan things like that.

But she hadn't really known much about gardening, and she worked full-time at a real estate agency—doing paperwork, administrative stuff—and she didn't have the time to learn. Which is not to say that she hadn't bought about a dozen books on gardening and printed several articles off the internet on the topic.

Even though she hadn't really known what she was doing, she had planted a garden their first spring in the house. She had thought of it as sort of a practice go round, a way of learning the ins and outs of the natural world so that when the first of those two babies came along, she would be ready. But the garden was weak. Sometimes the flowers didn't bloom at all, and when they did, they didn't look right, not the big, beautiful images of perfection she had seen on the little seed packets she had picked out.

And when she carried her coffee mug out into the yard on that first night after she met the man, the sight of the sparse garden—its speckles of feeble flowers and its huge patches of empty earth—filled her with a bubbling nausea. It was shameful, really, to have bought a house with such a wonderful yard and to fill it with such a halfhearted attempt at a garden. Seemed like it said something about Liz, about who she was deep inside.

No, she thought, this was not acceptable behavior. Like having a baby and never learning the proper way to feed it, hold it, raise it so it can deal with the world. She put her coffee mug on the patio and walked into the garden, started at the far corner and crouched down, grasped onto a little yellow dandelion—a dandelion, but she hadn't planted dandelions—and yanked it up by the roots. She looked around the garden, really looked for the first time in she didn't know how long. There were several dandelions, and some little purple things that she hadn't planted either. The ones that she hadn't

163

planted were the ones that looked the strongest, the ones whose blossoms were full and beautiful.

Weeds.

They must be choking the life out of the plants she had wanted to be there, had carefully picked out and planted one by one with her own hands.

She tossed the dandelion onto the ground and then moved on to the next living thing, and the next, pulling up clumps of flowers and weeds and tossing them into small piles on the earth. By the time Toby got up, she had uprooted every flower and plant in the garden that she could find and was raking them into a giant pile of detritus in the center.

Toby held a coffee mug in both hands the way actors do on TV, like there's something sacred about a morning cup of coffee. He cleared his throat, she supposed as a gesture of politeness. A way of letting her know she wasn't alone. But she didn't acknowledge it because if he wanted to say something he should just say it, for christ's sake. No more of this polite "hmm"ing and "well"ing like he was prone to do. Easing into a topic. Trying to respectfully broach the subject of whether or not she was insane.

He moved his mug to one hand and stepped over to her, reached out and locked his free hand around her elbow, the way the police do with crazy people or drunk people or old people who don't remember who they are. "Liz," he whispered and it felt as though he believed that she was still asleep and he didn't want to wake her, not yet.

She stopped raking and looked at him. Smiled. It wasn't what her instinct told her to do. Her instinct told her to rip her elbow free from his grip and yell. Howl, really. Tell him not to touch her, that he had no right to touch her, just because he was married to her he thought he had the right. But she didn't. She smiled. Smiled and said, "Morning, Toby."

He dropped his hand from her elbow and wrapped it back around his coffee mug. "You okay?"

She laughed and it came out in one sharp, "Ha!" She looked back down at the pile of dead things on the ground and then back at Toby. "Just couldn't sleep, I guess. Had a nightmare."

He took a sip of his coffee and let his eyes roam around the garden, resting, finally, on the pile of flowers at her feet. "Nightmare, huh?"

"Yeah, you know," she said. "Just a nightmare. Just your typical, run of the mill, garden variety nightmare." She laughed like before, only twice this time, "Ha ha!" and she half expected him to join in with her—ha ha ha, garden variety, that's a good one—but he didn't. Just kept standing there and looking at her and looking, too, at the pulverized garden. Trying, she could tell, to make sense of it all.

She told him about the nightmare, which was already becoming a vague memory in her mind, and about waking up after it, about seeing him and thinking he was the man. There was really more that she didn't tell him than she did. She didn't tell him about the death side of the vision, or about his part in the whole thing, and she didn't tell him about the blood. Didn't think he would understand something she didn't understand herself. All she told him, if you really want to boil it down, was that she needed to sleep alone for a while. Having a man's presence in the room scared her more than it made her feel safe. And so the second night, after a day spent out in the garden— because she wasn't ready to go back to work, but neither was she ready to just give in and wallow—she moved into the guest room for a temporary stay that both she and Toby knew could become permanent.

*

165

She had gotten off without so much as a warning, without even a reprimand or a "Don't even think about doing it again." They called it self-defense. She had wondered if she might have to go to court, if there would be a trial and a jury and if she would be forced to stand in front of hundreds and hundreds of staring eyes and explain herself. But no. Of course not, they said. It was obvious what had happened.

He had killed twelve other women before he had made a go at Liz. "Just a real creep," one of the cops told her. "A real crazy, if you know what I mean."

There were so many police officers. Liz hadn't cared enough to count, but they had simply surrounded her at the station, and they were eating—breakfast sandwiches and bagels, not a donut in the bunch—and sipping coffee from mugs that said things like, "Cops do it with the safety on," and "Number One Lover," and "Precinct 12 Fitness Day Champ 1999." 1999. And all these years later he was still drinking from the same cup, like if he stopped, packed it away and moved on, Fitness Day 1999 and his victory on that day would just fade into nothing; no one would remember, so he wouldn't be the champ anymore.

"Truth is, you did the world kind of a favor," the Champ told her. His belly pressed out against his button-up shirt. She wondered what he had looked like on Fitness Day in 1999, and what he saw when he looked in the mirror now. If he saw what she saw as she looked at him—his sagging stomach and his developing double chin—or if he still saw the man who had won that coffee mug, if he believed he was and always would be the Champ.

"No doubt about it," said one of the other cops, a tall, lean one who was eating a power bar and not drinking any coffee. "You're sort of a hero, really."

The other cops around her nodded and murmured their assent, and for a moment she thought they might burst into applause. She wouldn't know what to do if they did, wouldn't know if she was supposed to stand up and take a goddamned bow or what, so she was relieved when they didn't.

"A hero," Toby had said when she told him about it on the drive home. "My wife the hero."

*

She hadn't wanted to go back to work for the first two days, but she decided to come back somewhere in the middle of the third. She wasn't really doing anything at home, anyway. Once she had bagged up all the junk from the garden and set the bags—three of them, just bursting full—on the curb, there had been nothing else for her to do but sit and stare at the empty garden, rocking back and forth on the patio rocking chair and getting up periodically to freshen her coffee.

She didn't feel like cooking and she didn't feel like cleaning. She didn't feel like doing anything, and that included work, of course. But sitting there doing nothing wasn't proving to be a very good idea, either. There was nothing to keep her mind from straying to the man, to his hands on her body as he had felt around, squeezing her breasts like he was testing the ripeness of melons, turning her head this way and that to inspect her hair, her ears, her eyes and lips.

She would never know what he had been checking for, and that was just as well. Whatever it was it had been something crazy, something disturbed, no doubt. And whatever it was, he had been satisfied with her. He had even said something to that effect, "Yep, this'll do," or something like that in his gravelly voice. He sounded like an old man, she had thought at first, but then she realized what he really sounded like was a smoker. A man who had given in for too long to vice and habit, and whose throat—and breath—were paying the price.

167

She didn't want to remember it. Didn't want to think about what he had planned to do with her, but it was impossible not to because he had told her his entire plan. What he was going to do with her body before he killed her and then what he would do with her corpse after. He had ticked it all off like a list, "First I'm gonna . . . then I'll . . ." She had just sat there, her arms bound to the chair with scratchy twine, thinking, *You sick fuck. You sick fucking piece of shit*, her hands clenched into tight fists, her fingernails digging into the palms of her hands.

By that point, she had no longer been scared. Not really. The emotion she had felt right then had been anger. She almost hadn't cared if he was going to kill her, as long as she could inflict some pain on him first.

And that was why she had to go back to work: to stop her mind from replaying it over and over and over and . . . because she had lived through it once, goddamn it, and she didn't want to live through it again and again. Didn't want to sit out here every day for the rest of her life, staring out at the blank plot of earth and thinking about the rage she hadn't even known until three days ago was lying dormant inside of her.

So she called and told Ann, her supervisor, that she would be in tomorrow and to please let everybody know that she was fine. She was fine, she said, but she didn't want to talk about it. Please ask everyone not to bring it up. After she hung up with Ann she kept imagining it: Ann calling an all-staff meeting, giving a pep talk. Ann would say something like, "We are all so proud of our Liz and we probably all want to ask her questions or congratulate her or just tell her we're glad she's okay. But we all need a little normalcy in our lives. We all just want to be left alone sometimes. So let's all respect Liz's privacy."

That seemed okay, she thought, but then she thought about the questions they would ask Ann. Yes, of course, since they couldn't ask Liz, they would ask Ann. They would probably want to know, for starters, if Ann knew about how Liz had done it—the paper had been vague on the issue because Liz had been vague when the lady had interviewed her. Liz had fought the urge to tell the lady to get that fucking tape recorder out of her face, and she thought maybe she deserved some leniency, then, for responding in quick yes and no answers and short, enigmatic sentence fragments.

And when Ann told everybody that no, no, in fact, Liz hadn't said anything about that, they would want to know what Liz had said, exactly. And how did she sound? And did Ann think it would be appropriate to circulate a card, nothing specific on it, just something basic. Welcome back, Liz, and we love you.

Ann, who was nice to a fault, would probably close her eyes and think about it for a moment, and then say that she couldn't see any harm in that. And it would go from there. They would form a committee, take donations, oh god, they would decorate her desk with flowers and balloons and they would buy her a giftcard to the makeup counter at Meg's, like she really had any interest anymore in making herself more appealing to the rougher sex.

She sat on the rocker outside and stared out at the emptiness, trying to get her voice to a pitch that sounded steady. She practiced it, saying to the vacant yard, "Ann, I changed my mind. Ann, I have to change my mind. Ann, I'm sorry, but I think I changed my mind." When her voice sounded right, she stood up and went back into the kitchen. Without giving herself a second to reconsider, she dialed Ann's office and waited for the voicemail to beep.

"Ann, it's Liz again. Listen, short notice and all that but I have to change my mind about coming back tomorrow. I'm fine. It's nothing to worry about or anything. I just think,

169

well I've done some thinking, is what I'm trying to say, and I'm actually not sure that I'm going to come back at all." And then she said, "I'm sorry. I'm really, really sorry," and hung up.

*

Over dinner—burgers, again, because she hadn't felt like cooking, and grilling was all Toby knew how to do—she told Toby that she didn't think she wanted to go back to work. Toby took the news exactly as she expected he would, silently and without complaint. Although he did sort of wrinkle his brow, tap the edge of a potato chip against the side of his plate for a while, like he wanted to say something but couldn't decide whether he actually should.

She supposed it was possible that he wanted to ask her if she thought this was a good idea, if she didn't think it would be . . . prudent would be his word, to get back into a routine. It was possible, but she knew that wasn't what he wanted to say. What he wanted to say, she felt absolutely certain, was that maybe they should start trying. They had always planned on Liz quitting work one day, so she could stay home and take care of the babies. Whenever they began to have them. If she was going to quit work anyway, then now seemed like the perfect time. He had been doing well, just got a promotion two months before as a matter of fact, and now would have seemed like a good time, either way.

When he popped the chip into his mouth without saying anything, she felt relieved. He chewed the chip slowly, like he had decided that once he swallowed he would have to either speak now or forever hold his peace.

But she wasn't going to give him the chance. She stood up and carried her plate, which still had a half-eaten burger on it, to the trash, knocked its contents into the bin, and then placed it in the sink. "I can do the dishes tonight if you like," she said, already making her way back outside.

He swallowed his chip and said, "Don't even think it. I've got it." He stood up, even though he was clearly not finished himself, and carried his plate to the sink.

"Thanks," she said. "I'll be out back."

*

Liz had been working late that night, that would have been the punch line, if the whole thing had been a joke. And the funny thing was, she had chosen to be there late. Ann hadn't made her. She had been working on some project, the purpose of which she barely even remembered now—and that seemed funny, too—and she had sort of had her momentum going at quitting time. She couldn't stop, couldn't pause it, just like that, because if she did, she would have come home, made dinner, watched a late night movie, maybe, or played a board game with Toby, and by the time she got to work the next day, she would find herself stalling, checking her email, reorganizing the paper clips on her desk and telling herself she just wasn't feeling it today. So she had stayed late to make the most of it, to get the thing done while she felt like doing it.

And that had made it all the more dangerous because she had called Toby and told him that she didn't know when she would be home, told him that he shouldn't wait up. She had sealed her own fate, in a way, because nobody was expecting her and nobody would even notice that she was missing until the next day.

She supposed if she really thought about it that she could justify the whole thing like that. It was the desperation. It was that knowledge that this was her only hope. But it seemed like a stretch. Seemed like something a very bad person would tell herself when she had done something nobody could ever reasonably excuse.

*

As she sat in the rocker, staring out over the naked earth, something caught her eye. Something yellow. She squinted, because the sun was setting and the light was growing dim, but she knew full well what it was. Another dandelion. A weed.

She stood up and walked over to it, kneeled down, her knees sinking into the ground, and touched it, bent its stem this way and that to get a better look. Had she overlooked it, or had it sprouted up in these past three days? Perhaps it had been beginning to grow when she had decided to kill its brethren. Had it watched the carnage and decided to grow anyway, to stand tall and strong and defiant?

She dug her fingers into the earth and pulled it up, carried it to the garbage, and tossed it inside. She stepped back over to the dead garden and began walking around and around the edges of the empty soil, searching for any more lingering signs of life. She stopped when Toby came outside, wiping his hands with a kitchen towel.

"You wanna watch a movie or something?" he asked, fidgeting a bit with the towel, tossing it from one hand to the other and then folding and unfolding and refolding it again.

Of course she didn't want to watch a movie. Or something. She wanted to hunt around the dirt and make sure there was nothing left. She wanted to salt the earth to make sure there never would be. "Fine," she said, and it came out gruff, not at all how she had intended it. It was just that she suspected—hell, she knew—that he was worried about the garden thing.

Thought it was some sort of obsession, an unhealthy one, one that was holding her back from moving on.

He had never asked her about it. Probably figured he had let his chance slip by because he should have asked that first night, when he came out and found her at 4 a.m. raking up the remains of the war she had waged against nature. Even Liz acknowledged that he should have asked about it then. But he hadn't, and now it would be absurd for him to bring it up. Would seem like it had been on his mind this whole time, which it surely had been.

Part of the problem, too, was that she knew whatever he was thinking was probably right. She probably was obsessed, and not in a good way. This was her way of avoiding something that, really, it would be much healthier just to face. Face it and move past it. But she wasn't ready for what she was sure was Toby's sort of moving on. To start trying to get pregnant like they had always said they would one day do.

"I think we should make some popcorn and curl up on the couch under a blanket. Just zone out," Toby said, but it wasn't really what he wanted to say, she was sure of it.

She knew the baby issue was just a sentence away from tumbling out of his mouth and there would be no way to make him understand. Having kids was the natural order of things. It was animal instinct. It was not something she wanted to do anymore. She couldn't explain it any more than that. Something had changed inside her. She had wanted kids before the man, and after him she didn't, just like she had wanted a garden before they bought the house and now the sight of that brazen yellow flower made her feel vulnerable. And angry. She wanted to beat the earth and yell at it. "I control this garden. Me! This is my yard and I say what grows here and what doesn't."

But instead she walked inside with Toby, sat on the couch as he made some popcorn, and then stared blankly at the screen for an hour and a half, trying not to think about the empty garden outside and the weeds she could picture sprouting up in it. After the movie, Toby wanted to know if Liz still needed to sleep alone. "It's hard to sleep without you," he said and then added, "I miss you."

"I miss you too," she said. "But I'm not ready."

She tried not to see the disappointment on his face when he said, "I understand."

She slinked off to the guestroom and lay flat on her back on top of the covers. This is how it's going to be from now on, she told herself. Neither one of us saying what it is we mean to say.

*

Liz lay awake rolling onto one side, then the other, then onto her back, her stomach, her side again. Every time she closed her eyes she saw them, the dandelions, popping up and up and up all over the garden. She fought the urge to step outside and check, make sure the earth out there was still bare. It was ridiculous, she knew. Even weeds didn't grow that fast. Still, she couldn't close her eyes. Couldn't stand to see them in her mind, bright yellow petals shaped up into a smirk, laughing at her.

"This is crazy," she said aloud and rolled onto her back again, staring up at the ceiling. And a voice in her head responded: *No it isn't. You've seen crazy. You want me to remind you what crazy is?*

She sat up, swung her legs over the side of the bed and rubbed her bleary eyes. "This is crazy," she said again to the room, just to prove to herself that she still had the upper hand here. She still got to decide what she thought and what she didn't.

174

She tiptoed out of the room and down the hall, out the backdoor and into the yard. *I'm just going to make sure,* she promised herself. *I just need to see it with my own eyes and then I can get some sleep.* But it wasn't enough. After she squinted, let her eyes adjust to the moonlight, and then looked around the blank plot of earth, saw that there was nothing there, she didn't feel satiated like she had hoped she would. She had to look a second time and then a third. She had to turn on the porch light and fish a flashlight out from the shed, to crawl around the dirt on her hands and knees in a snaking line. She had to stick her fingers into the soil here and there, dig them in and make sure nothing was growing just beneath the surface.

*

The man had come up behind her and thrown a burlap sack over her head. Such a simple, uninspired way of doing it. Frightening, more than anything, because it wasn't particularly frightening. And she hadn't known what was happening at first. She had just been walking to her car, listening to her heels clack against the asphalt, and then suddenly everything was dark and she felt dizzy, felt her body lifting into the air and floating.

She had thought that she had passed out. That she had fallen and hit her head and this was all a dream. But then he tossed her into the trunk of his car, and her head banged against the lid as he slammed it down. The pain, more than anything, let her know she was still awake. When she recognized the sound of a car's engine—felt the familiar lurching of her stomach as the car backed up, then moved forward—she began to realize what was happening.

She had little space in the cramped trunk and she gave up quickly on freeing herself from the sack. All she could do was wait. As terrified as she was of where the stranger was taking her and why, she was anxious for the drive to end because she was beginning to feel nauseated from the movements of the car. The pounding of her heart and the quickness of her breath were almost worse than just facing whatever she was being taken to face.

Eventually, the car pulled to a stop, the engine shut off, and she heard a door open, slam shut again, and then, footsteps working their way around to the trunk. She took a deep breath. She didn't know who she was dealing with here, or what he intended to do with her, but no matter what, she knew the smartest thing she could do now was get that damn sack off her head and run.

When the lid of the trunk popped open, she sprang into action. Without even pausing to tear the sack from her head, she lunged forward and slammed into what she assumed must be a stomach. "Oof." Jackpot! She lunged forward again and leapt out of the trunk, but with the sack still pulled over her eyes, she had no perception of how high to jump or how far to tilt her body and so, before she even realized what was happening, she felt her shins catch on the inside of the trunk and her upper body came tumbling down to the ground.

Oafish laughter.

As she frantically tried to free her legs from inside the trunk, firm hands hefted her up by her armpits, the way she remembered being carried as a child. It had always been painful and it was even worse now, with fingers pressing forcefully into the sides of her breasts. He set her down and then lifted her back up again, this time slinging her over his shoulder.

She was floating again but this time had the wherewithal to lift the sack off of her head and drop it to the moving ground beneath her. She looked around. Trees, a thick forest of them, and brown parched grass. She thought about diving into it, kicking her legs and trying to loosen the man's tight grip, but she didn't think it would do her any good. For one thing, she probably couldn't get enough leverage to get away, and even if she could, he would surely catch her immediately. She didn't even know where she was. Didn't know if there was anywhere to run to, anywhere to hide.

He carried her into a garage, with its door open wide, and kept her tilted over his shoulder as he grabbed something— twine, she would find out soon enough—and then sat her roughly onto a metal chair. He began wrapping the twine around her body, pinning her arms to her side and securing her to the chair, and that was when he began telling her, between animal-like grunts, what he would do to her: "Grmph. First I'm gonna get you settled in this here chair. Grmph. And then I'll go over here and get my trusty hatchet. Grmph."

He wrapped the entire ball of twine around her and the chair, pulled it so tight she worried her ribs might crack, and then tied it deftly in place behind her back. He stepped back, at first she assumed to admire his handiwork, but she quickly realized it was to inspect her. He lifted his hand to her chin, tilted her head this way and that, reached out and touched her all over. He unbuttoned her blouse, lifted her skirt as high as the twine he had enveloped her in would allow, pressed parts of her skin so hard he left her body speckled in bruises, and all the while he kept grmphing with his raspy voice.

And after he was satisfied, he said whatever he said, "Yep, this'll do," or something like that. Then he stood up and walked to what the police would later refer to as his "workstation" and picked up a hatchet, tested its sharpness against his thumb, and then carried it back over to her chair. She stared straight ahead at a full-length mirror, which was leaning against the wall opposite her, as he kneeled down in front of her, laid the hatchet at his side, and reached forward to begin lifting her skirt.

In the mirror she could see his back, his broad shoulders, his short cropped hair with a swirling bald spot in a perfect circle on the crown of his head. His sunburnt neck. She looked down at his neck from the front. The pink skin heaved with every thick breath he took. He tilted his head to the side as he worked her skirt under each bit of twine, meticulously lifting the fabric higher and higher.

A vein pulsed beneath his skin.

Without pausing to think, she lunged forward, taking the entire chair with her, wrapped her teeth around his neck and bit down hard. She heard his flesh rip, his blood gurgle. Felt it trickle over the edges of her mouth and down her throat, inside her. She didn't mean to, didn't know where it came from, but she heard herself softly growling as she gnawed on his skin. His body went limp, then tumbled to the ground at her feet.

The thrill of survival was indescribable. *That bastard. That fucking piece of shit. Ha ha!* She threw her head back and laughed so hard, tears streaked down her cheeks and her belly started to ache. Laughed so hard she thought she would never stop. *I showed him. Didn't I? Didn't I? I fucking showed him!*

She kept right on laughing until she looked back out across the garage, looked into that goddamned mirror and caught her own wild gaze. Registered the blood dribbling over her chin. The chunks of flesh caught in her teeth. The growling sound that was still stealing out from somewhere inside.

*

By the time Toby woke up, by the time he came outside and found Liz skulking around the garden, she had already excavated the entire plot of ground. She had dug up all the soil, sifted it through her fingers, and then dropped it back onto the ground in little mounds. And she hadn't found a single dandelion.

When he came outside he found her pacing in a wide square, walking the entire edge of the land and kicking up the dirt with her once blue slippers, which had turned completely brown. She looked up at him when she heard his footfall. He stood for a moment staring blankly at her. "Liz?" he said cautiously, and reached out for her.

She smiled at him. "Toby," she said through a yawn. "I had to make sure there were no more weeds. This garden was drowning in weeds."

He looked around the upturned earth. "Those pretty yellow flowers?"

She tilted her head and her mouth dropped slightly open. She turned her head and looked around the empty ground and then looked back up at Toby, but she didn't say anything.

He shrugged. "Well, it's your garden. You getting it ready to plant something new?"

She inspected his face, his sleepy eyes, his hand still stretched out toward her, and she smiled again. A small smile, it only involved the edges of her lips, but she hoped he would see it nonetheless. "I don't know what I want to do yet," she said and stepped over to take his hand. And then, "I think I'm going to go back to bed. I didn't get much sleep." She stepped up to him and kissed him on the cheek.

He nodded. "You do look tired."

"I am," she said. "I'm very, very tired." She walked inside and started to walk to the guestroom but paused. She glanced back over her shoulder, saw Toby standing out on the porch, still looking out at the churned earth. She turned and walked into the bedroom, climbed under the covers and rested her head on Toby's still warm pillow, and then she closed her eyes.

PETER NEVER CAME

The thing that really got me wasn't the way he kept clearing his throat like he was trying to get my attention, or the way his eyes shifted around the room, stopping on the egg timer but then moving away again, as though he could actually convince himself there was anything else on his mind. What got me was the way he kept peeling the soap scum from the edge of the bathtub in long strips, then rubbing it into tubes between his thumb and forefinger. It was a compulsion, I guess. A disgusting one, and vulgar.

I leaned the back of my head against the mirror and said, "Did I ever tell you that I used to believe in Peter Pan?" I was sitting on the counter, my feet dipping into the dirty sink, and I closed my eyes. The squalor of our neglected bathroom was nauseating, and I didn't want to look at it anymore. Didn't want to look at him turning that goddamned grime into a toy. "I left my window open every night hoping against hope that he would come and take me away."

He cleared his throat again, and I opened my eyes. "You mean you pretended to believe. Like a game," he said, peeling another bit of the scudge off of the porcelain.

"No, really," I said. "I honestly believed. I wanted to be swept away to the Neverland. I would sit by the window all night." He didn't say anything and so I added, "Some kids pray to God, I prayed to Peter Pan." My body was twisted into a sort of pretzel, and my back was beginning to ache. It took my mind off of everything.

The tube of soap scum in his hand began to crumble. He stood up and tossed it in the garbage, then looked at me. "Sooner or later we're going to have to talk about this."

"About my love of Peter Pan?"

He frowned.

"I'm just kidding."

The thing about the soap scum was it made me feel ashamed. I had been meaning to clean the bathroom for I don't know how long. I just hadn't gotten around to it, so it just kept getting dirtier and dirtier. And the longer I put it off, the bigger the job became in my mind. The bathroom got to be so filthy I knew it would take a lot of time and effort to clean, and I knew, too, that I would have to just clean it again the next week, and the next. It was the perfect metaphor, really. But he would never understand.

"Well?" he asked.

"Well what? I don't know that there's anything to talk about."

"What does that mean?" He sat back down on the edge of the bathtub.

"It means I've already decided. I mean, if there's even anything to decide about."

He glanced at the egg timer again and said, "It isn't like it's just up to you."

I leaned forward to stretch my back and didn't say anything.

"We need to talk about this," he said.

"Don't worry," I said.

"I'm not," he said. "Not really." He looked at my hair in the mirror, like he didn't actually want to look right at me but he didn't want to look away, either. "How much longer?"

I knew he wanted me to check the egg timer, even though he had just looked at it seconds before, but instead I picked up the empty box and glanced at the back. And even then it was sort of a phony gesture. I had the instructions practically memorized. "It takes up to three minutes."

"But it might be less?"

"I guess."

"Well shouldn't we be checking it? I mean, what if it's already done?"

"You can. I think I'd rather wait." I kind of thought that getting up and looking at it over and over again would just make us both even more anxious. I didn't want him to check it either. I just suggested it because I figured he wouldn't want to touch it, for obvious reasons.

"I guess we can just wait," he said.

It kind of irritated me that he didn't just come out and say that he didn't want to touch it. I mean, it wouldn't have hurt my feelings or anything.

"Why didn't you want to grow up?" he asked. I could hear in his voice that it was a concession, his asking. It was him being willing to talk on my terms, but the war wasn't over. The war had only just begun.

I shrugged. "Everything is better when you're a kid. You're never bored, except when you have to go to sleep or take a bath or something. And then you're miserable. Feel like you're missing all the fun. Now it's like the only time I'm really happy is when I'm sleeping or taking an hour long shower."

I expected him to read something into my answer. To take it as the masked insult it probably subconsciously was. But he just nodded, even looked kind of pensive, and said, "So I guess you like kids?"

Ah. So this was his plan. I shrugged. "I don't want one of my own."

But he seemed not to have heard me and he folded his arms and leaned his side against the wall. "Well I think maybe it's about time, anyway. Lots of people our age have two or three by now."

Our age. I hate that. It's like being condemned for something you had no control over to begin with. Besides, it's not like we were that old. Just because everybody else was doing it and everybody seemed to wonder why we weren't, that didn't mean that we had to go along with it. Like when he would drag me to a party, which would normally be a cocktail party or a dinner party with tons of couples and a separate room where the kids were watching cartoons. And right when I felt like I was starting to relax and could maybe enjoy myself, someone would come up and put their left hand on my shoulder with their gaudy wedding ring sticking out and say, "So when are you two going to get married?"

He would always chuckle with that lame party laugh he's developed over years of being grown-up and say something about how he's just waiting for the right moment. Like that's all there was to it. He was just going to ask and of course I would say yes. And even worse was when the person would give me this consoling look, like, 'Oh you poor thing, you must be going crazy waiting.'

If I had been braver or wittier or bitchier, I would have made some biting remark about how he might be waiting for the right moment, but I was waiting for the right guy. But then everybody would have just felt even sorrier for me, like I was just trying to deal with being single still while everybody else was starting families. I think I would have had a better time at those things if they would have let me go to the other room and watch movies with the kids.

Anyway, he crossed his legs and started to jiggle his foot the way he does when he gets nervous. That's at least one thing I know about him for absolutely sure. Something he doesn't even know about himself, I think. His anxiety has these telltale signs that give him away when he's trying to act all collected and laidback. And the way he was jiggling his foot, I could tell he had something that he wanted to say. But I knew, also, that as long as his foot kept moving I was okay because it meant he was still nervous and wasn't ready to say whatever it was. It was bound to be something bad. There was nothing that he could say right then that wouldn't be.

All the different possibilities paraded around in my head. He might want to break up. And I didn't want that. I didn't want to marry him, but I still wanted to be with him. He might want to have the kid, and that would be worse than being dumped. Or maybe he wanted me to have the kid and put it up for adoption, which would just piss me off worse than anything because it's like saying, "I don't want to have to deal with it, but I think that you should still go through all that pain and fatness and everything just to avoid my conscience being burdened." I made up my mind that if he asked me to do that I would just tell him to fuck off. That kind of thing makes it easier because whenever you get down about it you can just remember that awful thing he said right before the end and feel better off.

His foot stopped moving and my stomach went cold. "I don't really like kids," I said quickly.

His foot started jiggling again. "Not at all?"

"Not even a little bit." This wasn't completely true. I do kind of like kids. Sometimes, anyway. They're cute and sweet and fun, when they're not being little terrors. But the thing is, I wouldn't want one of my own. Because when it's someone else's kid, you can just hang out with them when they're being adorable and give them right back to their parents when they start crying or wetting the sofa or breaking things. And if they break something of yours, their parents are always so apologetic and they pay for it if you want them to, and if you don't then they think you're some kind of an angel for being so understanding. Half the time it was just some ugly vase your boyfriend's sister bought you for Christmas and you're happy to be rid of it because if you had thrown it out yourself, he would have had a fit, going on about how she didn't have to get you anything and blah blah blah.

"This is something we should talk about," he said. "Even if you aren't . . . you know." Oh God, he couldn't even bring himself to say it. Here he was trying to act like the adult and he couldn't even say this one measly little word. "I mean we've never really talked about it before."

I sighed. "What do you want to talk about?"

"Well, I want kids. I wasn't planning on having one right now, but I do want to have them someday. Are you saying you don't ever want to have any?"

I looked him right in the eye and said it: "I don't ever want to have kids. Ever. Besides, I'd make a lousy mom."

But I shouldn't have added that last bit because of course that was the part he latched on to. "You'd make an amazing mother," he said as he stood up and stepped over to me, lifted my chin in what I'm sure he meant to be a reassuring gesture. "You're great with kids."

I pulled my chin away. "It doesn't matter because I don't want to have any," I said. "I don't like them."

He stepped back and cocked his head. "Could have fooled me."

"I just don't want to have any, okay? It's just not something that," I twisted my hand around in the air, searching for the words, "interests me."

185

"But you say it like it's something that people choose to do because it's interesting," he said. "I just assumed you wanted kids. Everybody wants kids."

"Apparently not everybody." I curled my toes up in the sink and watched them relax again. The sink was even dirtier than the rest of the bathroom, filled with little black hairs from when he'd shaved his goatee off. It was repulsive. I wanted to tell him to clean it, but I didn't want to get into all that. It's so boring, fighting about things like cleaning up after yourself or turning the lights off when you leave the room.

"The thing is," he said, "it isn't just you here, you know? We're in this together. You can't just decide that we're not ever going to have kids and not even take my feelings into consideration."

"Fine, how do you feel about it?"

"I feel that our lives will be significantly less full if we don't have a family. I also think you, well both of us, will regret it when we start getting older and we don't have any kids to come visit us. No memories of family holidays."

I gave him a second to add any additional evidence to the pile, but that seemed to be it, so I said, "Is that all?" I immediately wished I hadn't, though, because his mouth contorted and his eyes got all wide. I could tell I had hurt his feelings, but I figured I may as well keep going. "Because I have very strong feelings about it, too, you know. I feel that you shouldn't be forced into parenthood if it's not what you want for your life. I think being a parent isn't something that you should just do to make someone else happy."

He shifted his weight from his right foot to his left and looked down. I figured he was thinking about what he had wanted to say earlier.

The dirt and the grime from the bathroom walls felt like they were closing in around us, and the whole situation started to feel unreal. For no reason I could explain to him I wanted to start talking about Peter Pan again. I wanted to explain to him what I knew he could never understand. That there was something special about that book. It was just so right on. Even when I was a little kid I had known it was true. Being grown-up isn't worth it.

He stepped up to the counter. I had my hands laced around my legs, and he peeled them apart and held them in his own, much bigger hands. It felt good but in a sad way, like when you realize at her funeral how much your grandmother loved you.

He kissed the knuckles on my right hand, then my left, then said, "I love you."

I wanted to jerk my hands back. It's not like it was the first time he had said it, but it felt different this time. It felt like he meant it. Instead of ripping my hands away or running screaming from the room, I dropped my head onto my knees and started to cry. He let go of my hands and wrapped his arms around me and started kissing me all over my face and even in my hair. He kept saying it over and over, "I love you, I love you," and every time he said it, I just felt a little more like I wanted to die.

"I can't do this," I said. "I just can't."

"It's okay. I'm here."

"If it's positive I'm going to have an abortion."

I felt his muscles tighten, but he kept holding me and kissing me so he must not have been too upset. "We'll talk about it later."

"I don't want to talk about it at all."

He pulled away and put his hands in my hair, then looked into my eyes and got that intense expression that guys get when they think they're being romantic. I hate that expression more than anything in the world. Like, when he was holding me and kissing my hair and saying, "I love you," over and over again, it was kind of nice because it felt good and all, but at the same time it made me cry even harder. Because it just wasn't real.

So he had that look on his face and he cleared his throat again and said, "I think we should get married."

It was just like him to say it like a statement rather than a question. Like how he had supposedly been waiting for the right moment and now that it was here he would just let me know so I could go all gushy. Only I didn't go all gushy. The truth is I felt sort of sick.

"What do you think?" He still had that horrible look on his face.

For a second I was afraid I might actually throw up. "I don't know."

"What do you mean you don't know?" He let go of my head and stepped back, crossing his arms.

"I mean I've never really thought about it." That was true, although I probably shouldn't have said it because he looked so hurt I thought he was going to start crying now.

"Not even a little?"

"I'm sorry," I said. "I don't think I want to get married."

"Not to anyone?"

"If I don't want to marry you, why would I want to marry someone else?" I thought that would make him feel better, but I guess I said it kind of unsympathetically and he actually did cry. I think he did, anyway. He turned away from me, and when he turned back he was wiping his eyes. Maybe he just wanted me to think he was crying.

"I guess I just always thought we would get married and have kids one day. Look, if you're worried that I'm just saying it because . . . I mean, if you think I don't really mean it, don't worry. I've been thinking about proposing for a while."

"I don't think that you're just saying it because of all this." I did. "I just don't think I want to get married. I don't want to have kids and I don't want to get married."

"Alright," he said slowly. "So then, where do you see this going?"

"What?"

"Us."

"What do you mean?"

"You know what I mean. I want to marry you. I want you to have my babies. I want us to have a family and I want to be with you forever."

That sort of talk makes my stomach turn, but I couldn't tell him that, not right when he was pouring his heart out about it all. "I just don't think this is something we should rush into."

"Rush into?" he said. "We've been together for almost a year, and we're not getting any younger. So, now you're telling me that this whole time you never had any intention of making a commitment to me?"

"I'm sorry." Lame, I know, but I didn't know what else to say. I wasn't going to back down, that was for damn sure.

"That's it? You're sorry. You wasted a year of my life and you're sorry?"

That was low. "I didn't realize you thought of it as such a waste," I said.

"Well, we're adults. You might not want to act like one, but I certainly do. I can't spend the rest of my life like this. I need commitment. I need security."

All of this mind-numbing chatter was starting to make my head hurt, and I was beginning to think maybe it was better if we did just break up. At least I wouldn't ever have to have another conversation like this. I wished I had never even told him about being late to begin with. If I had just taken the test alone and then handled the problem myself, none of this ever would have happened.

The egg timer dinged.

Neither one of us moved. We both just kept looking at each other, waiting, I guess, for the other to take the initiative.

Finally, I lifted my legs and draped them over the counter top. "Well," I said. "Here goes."

His expression softened a little, and he reached out and helped me down from the counter. I walked over to the back of the toilet and picked up the tester. I stared down at it for a second and then, when I felt his eyes boring into me, I handed it to him.

He gaped down at it. "What does it mean?"

"One bar is no. Two is yes."

"Oh." He handed it back to me, and I tossed it in the trash. "Do you think you should take the other one, just in case?"

The box had come with two. I didn't know if it was for the sort of girl who needed them on a regular basis or if it was to double check the first results. "I don't know. I'm sure it's right."

"I'm sorry," he said. "About what I just said. I didn't mean it. I love you and I don't think of one second that I've spent with you as a waste."

I nodded and looked down. I didn't want to look at him. Suddenly I wasn't sure how I felt about him anymore. I guess some things just can't be taken back.

"I understand about you not wanting to get married. I won't press it, but if you change your mind will you let me know?" He stepped forward to put his arms around me again, but I skirted around him before he had a chance and walked out the door and into the bedroom. He followed.

"Sure." I shrugged. I sat down on the bed and stared at the bookshelf.

"So what happens now?" He sat down beside me.

"I'm tired. I just want to go to bed."

"Are you mad at me?" he asked.

I sat for a second, staring straight ahead, before I finally said, "No."

"Do you still love me?" he asked.

I hate questions like that. I always want to say no, just because he asked. "Yes."

"Me too."

He put his arm around me and started kissing me again. I didn't much feel in the mood after all that, so I yawned right in the middle of a kiss. He must have gotten the hint because he just kissed me once more on the cheek and then lay down on the bed. He patted the spot next to him and I lay down, too, but I had lied. I wasn't really tired.

He fell asleep pretty quickly. He drops off faster than anyone I've ever known. I just lay there staring at the spot on the bookshelf where my copy of *Peter Pan* should've been, only it wasn't there. I don't remember if I had lent it to someone or lost it or what. Somehow that made me even sadder than everything else that had happened that night.

The window was open. It had been pretty hot the past few nights and we had never bothered closing it. That night it was kind of chilly, though, and the wind that blew in through the opening was starting to make me shiver. I stood up and slid the window shut, and then I started crying again. Not because of the fight or the test or even the fact that his mind was so simplistic he could just drop off to sleep like that while I lay awake mulling everything over. I was crying because

191

of that missing copy of Peter Pan. I hadn't read it in years, but it made me cry anyway.

I used to leave the window open every night when I was a kid. I'd leave it open all night and just wait for the boy who didn't know a kiss from a thimble and who could only play at love but never make it. I was so sure that he was out there, that he would come for me. But after a while the breeze from the open window had stopped being soft and inviting, cool and hopeful. After a while it had just become cold.

EPILOGUE

THE NUMBER ONE

On Friday, November 30th, 2007, at precisely 7:48 in the morning, Eastern Standard Time, Anna Kelsey McMillan became, for the duration of 5.3 minutes, the number 1 most beautiful woman in the world. 3 of those 5 minutes Anna spent in her car, alone, where nobody saw her in all of her splendor. But Anna spent 2 of those glorious minutes traversing the parking lot of the large business complex where she was expected, at 8 o'clock, to commence her presentation on farmed salmon.

3 people were in the parking lot with Anna during those 2 minutes. The first, Charles B. Abrams, was on his cell phone and hardly even noticed Anna as she passed by. The second person, Clarice Mandle, who was, that morning, having a self-described bad hair day and believed herself to be the number 1 ugliest woman in the world (though she was actually number 1,346,412,912 at that exact moment), noticed Anna and responded with an instinctive twinge of jealous spite. Fortunately, the third person in the parking lot that morning, John Quinn, not only noticed Anna but appreciated her dazzling beauty, her resplendent loveliness.

John was on his way to a meeting and his mind was bogged down with the endless streams of data he would soon be discussing with his coworkers. He had only just parked, just climbed out of his car, when he was blindsided by Anna's beauty.

As Anna passed, John mentally acknowledged that she was the most beautiful woman that he had ever seen (not knowing that she was, at that moment, the most beautiful woman period). Mesmerized, he dropped the briefcase he had been about to pull from his backseat and, instead, watched Anna strut away. No thought of his wife and how she might feel to know her husband was at that moment in a parking lot ogling another woman entered his mind. But his wife didn't know, and anyway, it wasn't as though there were anything sexual about it. No. John wasn't admiring Anna's plump frame, her soft brown curls, and her pale pink cheeks out of some animalistic response of arousal. She was simply beautiful; surely his wife wouldn't mind another glance.

John allowed himself to gaze for 4.6 seconds at the back of Anna's thick curls as she made her way towards the building before he climbed right back into his car and drove straight home to his own, he suddenly remembered, very attractive wife. When he would arrive home, 32.8 minutes later, he would take his wife in his arms and carry her to the bedroom, where they would have the $3{,}489{,}674{,}123^{rd}$ most passionate sex of all time. Afterwards he would call in sick to the meeting, but first things first.

John's wife would never know that it had been Anna that reminded her husband how much he loved her, nor that 43.7 seconds after John turned away from Anna, a swift breeze blew a mocha colored strand of hair into Anna's right eye (the same strand of hair which had, 5.3 minutes earlier, been wafted by her car's rogue air conditioner precariously close to her eye). Without missing a step, Anna puffed a blast of air from her lips upward, driving the hair out of her eye and making her the number $500{,}250{,}009^{th}$ most beautiful woman in the world, still no small accomplishment.

Anna didn't know that for 5 brief minutes she had been number 1, and so she didn't miss it. Instead, she made her way towards the building where she would demonstrate for her boss and a small committee of investors that she was the number 4,300,979th most knowledgeable person in the world on farmed salmon. Just that morning, she had been the 4,300,978th most knowledgeable, but as Anna was making her way to the parking lot, fiddling with her air conditioner and being beautiful, fifteen-year-old Suzie Ann Canfield of Phoenix, Arizona was looking up information on farmed salmon for a school report and had surpassed Anna in knowledge on that particular subject.

Had Anna known that a teenager knew more about her field than she herself did, she may have lost the resolve to give her presentation to these investors, whose money Anna's company very badly needed. She may have just not shown up, because she wouldn't, probably, have also known that Suzie would only remain ahead of her for 4 days; once Suzie handed in her report on Monday, the facts would begin drifting their way out of her brain, as facts are wont to do when they are being ignored.

But Anna didn't know and so she continued her confident stride to the building's entrance, as well she should have, because, after all, Anna was the world's 800,239,438th best knitter, the 4,124,345th most accomplished backgammon player, and had the 1,897,763rd largest collection of greeting cards.

And that, as we all know, is enough.

Ashley Cowger holds an MFA in Creative Writing from the University of Alaska Fairbanks and a BA in English from Northern Arizona University. Her short fiction has appeared in several literary journals and has been nominated for a Pushcart Prize. She teaches college English and is the editor and cofounder of the online journal, MFA/MFYou (www.mfamfyou.com). She has divided her life fairly evenly between Alaska, Arizona, and California, and has driven the historic Al-Can Highway twice. She currently lives in southeast Ohio with her husband, cat, and collection of overweight stuffed animals. Learn more at www.ashleycowger.com, where you can also participate in a virtual book club discussion about Ashley's stories.

Autumn House Fiction Series

New World Order by Derek Green
Drift and Swerve by Samuel Ligon*
Monongahela Dusk by John Hoerr
Attention Please Now by Matthew Pitt*
Peter Never Came by Ashley Cowger*

*Winners of the Autumn House Fiction Prize
Selected by Sharon Dilworth

Colophon:

Design by Rebecca King

Cover Art: "Mirrors" © 2010 by Ashley Gibson

Title font: Booter Zero-Zero © Apostrophic Labs.
Text font: Adobe Caslon Pro

Printed by McNaughton-Gunn on 60# Natural Offset.